'I absolutely loved this . . .
forever'

'A delectable second novel
people together, even across d
emotionally generous novel demonstrates how people's worlds can expand when they open themselves to new possibilities. Readers will be touched by this enriching tale and inspired to embark on their own international culinary adventures' *Booklist*

'This charming, effervescent little novel . . . deserves to be a huge bestseller' *Red Magazine*

'Fay's touch is deft . . . The story leaves the reader wanting more – more recipes, more letters, more time in the gentle, unfolding friendship of these two women. A glimpse into a friendship that doesn't hesitate to touch on joy, sadness, love, and death' *Kirkus Reviews*

'Unutterably delightful . . . a gentle escape to the past'
Shelf Awareness

'Part historical fiction, part friendship saga, and part carnival for the senses, *Love & Saffron* isn't just for food lovers – it's an ode to risk-takers, trailblazers, and the chefs in all of us. With lush descriptions of food and a resonant historical setting, *Love & Saffron* is a sweet, savoury, and emotional pleasure. It's like a dinner with friends you won't want to end'
J. Ryan Stradal, author of *Kitchens of the Great Midwest*

'In Kim Fay's charming novel, two women in 1960s Los Angeles and Washington State become the best of friends long before they meet in person. Together, they navigate relationships, ambition, societal expectations, and the arts of making and writing about food. Warm, delicious, and absolutely satisfying – I devoured it in one enthusiastic gulp!'
Meg Waite Clayton, author of *The Last Train to London*

'As refreshing as watching the sunset over the Pacific Ocean, with a glass of sauvignon blanc and a bowl of garlicky clams at your elbow. Kim Fay convincingly recreates a charming and civil world, and a touching friendship, in a period piece that will restore you to your kinder, gentler self'
Richard C. Morais, author of *The Hundred-Foot Journey*

'In the footsteps of Laurie Colwin and Ruth Reichl, *Love & Saffron* is a beautiful, gentle, intimate exploration of food and friendship, as well as life, loss, and love'
Susan Elia MacNeal, author of *Mr. Churchill's Secretary*

'A deliciously memorable and lovely story of friendship, food, and the enduring connections we form through the lost art of letter writing'   Tembi Locke, author of *From Scratch: A Memoir of Love, Sicily, and Finding Home*

'Utterly captivating from the first page to the last . . . Kim Fay has penned a touching, satisfying novel that readers will surely savour for a long time to come. This story will fill your heart, lift your spirit, and feed your soul. I truly didn't want it to end'   Heather Webber, author of *Midnight at the Blackbird Café*

'Simply a delight. In letters between two women – strangers, at first, but ultimately best friends – in 1963, Kim Fay reveals how a love of food can open doors into culture, history, homes, and love. Indulge yourself in the world of Joan and Immy, preferably with some quesadillas or mussels in wine and saffron by your side'

Ann Hood, author of *The Knitting Circle*

'A story about the joys of being alive – the delight found in discovery, the comfort of a good meal, and most of all, the richness of true friendship. It is a story about connection – to place, to food, and to each other. I read *Love & Saffron* in one delicious afternoon. It's the kind of story you get lost in, one that breaks you open, fills your heart, and reminds you of what is important in life. A genuine pleasure. You'll want to share it with everyone you call friend'

Louise Miller, author of *The City Baker's Guide to Country Living*

'Astonishing, exhilarating, existential! *Love & Saffron* explodes forever the arbitrary separation of fiction from fact. I inhaled this book in one delectably deep breath, uncovering layer after layer of the aromas, flavours, tastes on lips and tongue of my own life as a young American housewife in the 1960s. Author Fay conveys the texture of daily life as a mystery story that discovers food is a cultural creation and connector as powerful as storytelling itself to erase the separation of past from present and memory from now. This is a book for every person with a heart. READ IT NOW!'   Betty Fussell, author of *The Story of Corn*

ALSO BY KIM FAY

FICTION

The Map of Lost Memories

NONFICTION

Communion:
A Culinary Journey Through Vietnam

To Vietnam with Love:
A Travel Guide for the Connoisseur

To Asia with Love:
A Connoisseur's Guide to Cambodia,
Laos, Thailand, and Vietnam

LOVE &
SAFFRON

A Novel of Friendship,
Food, and Love

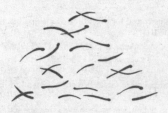

Kim Fay

First published in Great Britain in 2022 by Two Roads
An imprint of John Murray Press
An Hachette UK company

This paperback edition published in 2023

2

A CIP catalogue record for this title is available from the British Library

Paperback ISBN 978 1 529 39510 5
eBook ISBN 978 1 529 39511 2

Printed and bound in Great Britain by Clays Ltd, Elcograf S.p.A.

John Murray policy is to use papers that are natural, renewable
and recyclable products and made from wood grown in sustainable forests.
The logging and manufacturing processes are expected to conform to the
environmental regulations of the country of origin.

Two Roads
Carmelite House
50 Victoria Embankment
London EC4Y 0DZ

www.tworoadsbooks.com

for Janet Brown,

Barbara Hansen,

and my Great-Aunt Emma Ethier

"When shall we live, if not now?" asked Seneca before a table laid for his pleasure and his friends'. It is a question whose answer is almost too easily precluded. When indeed? We are alive, and now. When else live, and how more pleasantly than supping with sweet comrades?

— M. F. K. Fisher,

"Meals for Me," *Serve It Forth*

Love & Saffron

PART ONE

PART ONE

October 1, 1962
Los Angeles, Calif.

Dear Mrs. Fortier,

I hope this letter finds you well. For that matter, I hope it finds you, since I am sending it to <u>Northwest Home & Life</u> magazine, where I so enjoyed your recent tale about digging for clams. I laughed out loud at your smug heron and briny crown of kelp. I admire women who do not care if they look foolish in front of others, even though I am not one of them.

I am a dedicated reader of "Letter from the Island," and I send my congratulations for your ten-year anniversary as its author. I have known it from the beginning when I was seventeen. Mother loves her magazine subscriptions, and every month, as soon as they arrive, she folds back the pages to her favorite columns. The first two she reads are always yours and Gladys Taber's "Butternut Wisdom" in <u>Family Circle</u>. I prefer yours. It makes me feel like I am having a conversation with a good friend, and your enthusiasm for life has taught me to be more aware of my own world around me, and especially the outdoors. Believe it or not, Los Angeles has much to offer in the way of natural beauty if you pay close attention.

I notice you have written about mussels a few times, but you only ever mention cooking clams. I recently learned a creative mussels recipe from a Frenchwoman I met on a voyage to the Far East. I am enclosing a packet of saffron from that voyage. It is my small way of thanking you for "Letter from the Island."

For steamed mussels, in a stockpot add a generous pinch of saffron, coarsely chopped garlic, and parsley to a half cup melted butter. The red enamel pot you mentioned in your column about racing Dungeness crabs, the one with the pockmark from your niece's Red Ryder BB gun, will do perfectly. If you can't find fresh garlic, shallots can be substituted, but in my opinion, without fresh garlic the dish isn't worth making. The Frenchwoman told me the addition of a cup or so of white wine is considered standard for this broth, but she prefers vermouth. I agree with her. It gives the dish a crisp, botanical flavor, and I can save my Chablis for drinking with my meal.

Your not-so-secret admirer,

Miss Joan Bergstrom

FROM THE DESK OF MRS. IMOGEN FORTIER

October 12, 1962
Camano Island, Wash.

Dear Miss Bergstrom,

Greetings from the eye of the storm. Typhoon Freda churned to life a few days ago in the far reaches of the Pacific and got it into her stormy head to roar in our direction. I wonder, is she still a typhoon once she lands on American shores? Meteorological semantics isn't my area of expertise, and my trusty Britannicas are safely hunkered down on the shelves at home. Francis and I came out to the cabin for the Columbus Day weekend to pick mussels and try the saffron you so thoughtfully sent. Instead, we've been battening our hatches.

Apologies for the tottery penmanship. I didn't bring my typewriter with me since my intention was to write to you next week after I made your recipe with <u>great success</u>. Not only do I not mind looking foolish, I'm an optimist! Unfortunately, we didn't collect a single mussel, and I'm writing by the light of a kerosene lantern because the power has gone out.

I'm writing rather than pacing because my pacing

was driving Francis crazy. He finally told me to do something to take my mind off the storm. Easier said than done. This afternoon the sky turned black and filled with spectral yellow streaks, and now it feels like our wood-clad cabin will wash away at any minute. This isn't an unreasonable fear, considering it's old wartime housing that we had floated to its present location four years ago on a barge from the naval shipyard down west of Seattle. I've never experienced gales like this before, or maybe I have, but the windstorm of 1934 came at the height of the Depression when I was a weary housewife, feeling a thousand years old rather than the thirty-one I actually was, and my larder was down to a questionable jar of dried beef. A house blown off its foundation seemed like the least of our worries during those bleak times.

I tried reading but can't concentrate on the only unread novel here on our shelves. A Book of the Month selection, <u>Rabbit, Run</u>, by a self-satisfied-looking stuffed shirt named John Updike. It was left behind by my friend Hazel. After tormenting myself with a few morose chapters, I began to suspect Hazel abandoned it on purpose. While the storm could fairly be blamed for my lack of charity, I'm sure I would find this book a toil in clear weather, too. The protagonist gazes at his navel as if he is the first man in history to have feelings of dissatisfaction about his life. He doesn't have any interest at all in making the best of things. I wish I'd brought the new Nero Wolfe to read instead.

I hope you don't find it insulting that I'm using you for my mandated distraction. I do realize I'm rambling. I was pleased to receive the saffron, which I read about in an article by Elizabeth David. I think it was in <u>Gourmet</u>. Does she write for <u>Gourmet</u>? Or maybe it was in one of M. F. K. Fisher's delectable books, but now that I think about it, perhaps Freya Stark mentioned saffron in her writings about Persia. Rambling, indeed. Francis calls it my specialty and says that if I were paid for it, we'd be rich. Anyhow, at your mention of your Far East voyage, I immediately pictured you tall and most certainly elegant, draped in silk, perched on a camel in a spice bazaar. My fascination with <u>National Geographic</u> gives me a vivid imagination. I'm not an adventuress like you, though. My spirit and appetite wander extravagantly through the pages of books and magazines, but my body and stomach stick close to home with few exceptions, Canada and Glacier National Park, and a long-ago visit to San Francisco where I enjoyed chipeeno (I'm positive I'm not spelling that correctly) at the Old Clam House.

I close with a heartfelt thank-you for your intriguing gift and generous words about my column. I'm always surprised when I receive a fan letter, since I associate them with movie stars and grand authors like Edna Ferber and Pearl S. Buck. I've never considered myself a professional writer. Occasional vignettes in a garden club newsletter were seen by a former high school classmate in a position of editorial power, and voila! For a decade now, "Letter from the Island" has been a monthly staple in <u>Northwest Home & Life</u>. I send additional gratitude for giving me good reason to put pen to page while the wind whips, the windows shudder, and the roof shakes.

With warm regards,

Mrs. Imogen Fortier

P.S. My thanks, as well, to your mother for bringing my column into your home, and as a result, your gracious letter to me.

December 12, 1962
Los Angeles, Calif.

Dear Mrs. Fortier,

After I mailed my letter to you, I worried that you would consider it impertinent, especially the part where I gave you cooking advice, as if you of all people need advice on cooking shellfish. I was relieved when you replied, and with such kindness. It is my turn to thank you for providing me with a necessary distraction.

Your letter arrived with the Cuban crisis hot on its heels. There is an air-raid siren a block from my house, and Mother shouted a curse on the bald head of old Nikita every time it practiced wailing. Between the sirens and her outbursts, my nerves began to fray. Your mention of Elizabeth David reminded me of her recipe for risotto alla Milanese, which I have wanted to try for a long time. As I am sure was the case in your area, the grocery store shelves went bare as everyone prepared for end times. In a harebrained panic, I rushed to C & K Importing for their gallon cans of artichoke hearts, and by the time I got to the Mayfair, all the macaroni and bottled water were gone. Fortunately, I already had the ingredients for risotto in my pantry.

It was a balm to turn my attention to rice and butter. It was my own small way of rebuffing shattered nerves and the Reds, although I suppose hamburgers or hot dogs would have been a more appropriate form of patriotic resistance.

I made enough risotto to fuel the entire naval blockade. Instead, I invited the neighbors for dinner, along with their carpenter, Mr. Rodriguez, who was over building special cabinets for their fallout shelter. Everyone enjoyed it. Mrs. David's approach is to pound the saffron in a mortar and then steep it in broth before adding the liquid at the end of the recipe.

Regarding your comment about my looks, I am tall but hardly elegant, and as for my being an adventuress, while it is flattering, it is also untrue. I cannot begin to imagine traipsing into the woods to hunt for elk with your passel of sisters-in-law, as you described them in your column a few years back. Five women alone in the wild. That is adventure. I have simply always had an interest in people from other countries. I like the way their kitchens smell. At Stanford I was drawn to students from India because they cooked up little pots of curry in their rooms.

My Far East voyage came about through Mother's

friend Jean Bartel, who has traveled all over the world. She suggested that it would broaden my horizons, and Mother is a firm believer in this. Mrs. Bartel is a remarkable woman, a former Miss America. She even hosts her own travel program called It's a Woman's World. After my graduation, she made arrangements for a cabin for me on a Norwegian freighter and set up the land portions with lodgings in Hong Kong, Singapore, and Bangkok. There were twelve passengers on the ship. We were met by a representative at each port and fully escorted to restaurants and cultural sites. As you can see, it was a tame trip. Nor did I sit on any camels, since they are not found in that part of the world, but I did pet a well-behaved elephant named TipTop. I also bought beautiful shawls at the Thai Silk Company. It is the same company whose fabrics outfitted The King and I on Broadway.

The news reports about your Columbus Day storm were harrowing, and the photographs of the aftermath remind me of our earthquakes. I hope your cabin survived unscathed.

Your not-so-secret admirer still,

Miss Joan Bergstrom

P.S. I am also a Nero Wolfe fan, and I enjoy Simenon, as well. My favorite local writer of suspense novels is Charlotte Armstrong.

P.P.S. If you don't have Elizabeth David's <u>Italian Food</u> please let me know. I will copy the risotto recipe and send it to you.

From the Desk of Mrs. Imogen Fortier

January 5, 1963
Camano Island, Wash.

Dear Miss Bergstrom,

If you won't consider yourself an adventuress when it comes to travel, at least please admit that you're one in the kitchen. I'm glad my letter helped you weather the Cuban crisis. Up here in our soggy neck of the woods, I trembled in a state of shock, and Francis was struck with a violent migraine.

Men are such obvious creatures. During the storm he could do practical things to safeguard us, such as nail plywood over windows, secure the boat, etc. etc. During the standoff he could only sit glued to the radio and wait for Kennedy and Khrushchev's despicable game of double-dog dare to run its course. Women are groomed to accept a certain degree of helplessness, but men, especially men like Francis who fought face-to-face in the trenches, are unsettled I believe by this new, impersonal style of warfare. Maybe that's why I didn't like the John Updike novel I wrote about to you. It's selfish to have one of these faddish existential crises when there are so many more genuine concerns, like the next Hiroshima.

Francis and I finally tried your recipe, and I must fess up. We've never had mussels before. We always thought of them as freeloaders clinging where they're not wanted, and you must agree, their beards are unappetizing. What a small-minded misjudgment on our part. I didn't have garlic or even shallots, so I had to chop an Italian red onion. Mea culpa! But you're right about the vermouth. What a divine flavor. I will never look at those ebony shellfish the same way again.

I want to reciprocate. I don't have anything as exotic as saffron. I hope a jar of my blackberry jam will do. As you know, I write often about picking wild native blackberries. It's a chore since they're not easy game like the big purple bubbles that grow all over the sides of the road around here. Whenever I set out to hunt for a hidden patch in an old clear-cut, Francis accuses me of looking like a hobo with my canvas sunhat, khaki trousers, and Folgers cans tied over my shoulders. I don't care. When I'm in the brambles, I'm happy as a clam at high tide. Just writing to you about it makes me wish for July mornings. There's always a perfect moment when the sun strikes the bushes and a deep, sweet, earthy smell rises into the air.

Your mention of <u>Italian Food</u> gave me an excuse to drive into Seattle for a visit to Shorey's booksellers. They didn't have a copy on hand but assured me they will chase one down and mail it to me. In the meantime, I found a novel by Charlotte Armstrong. Have you read <u>The Seventeen Widows of Sans Souci</u> yet? If you have, please don't give anything away. Once I finish, I'll let you know and we can share our thoughts on it.

You also mentioned your neighbor's carpenter, Mr. Rodriguez. I believe there's a large Mexican population in Los Angeles. Despite my extensive culinary reading, my palate is embarrassingly sheltered. Can you recommend any Mexican recipes for me to try? Francis surprised me by how much he loved your broth for steamed mussels, not to mention how much he loved mussels, and your travels inspire me to become more international in the kitchen. After your saffron, the most exciting spice in my cabinet is paprika. What would a good American housewife's rotating dinner party repertoire be without Hungarian chicken? Mea culpa—again! We eat with scant creativity, grilling fish and roasting meat. Francis would live off cans of Dinty Moore beef stew if I weren't here to make pot roast. Like any couple married so long (forty years!), we're probably too set in our ways.

Thank you for allowing me the pleasure of rambling once again.

With warm regards,

Mrs. Imogen Fortier

P.S. Since you refuse the description adventuress, I propose cosmopolitan. After all, you're a city girl, as well as family friends with a former Miss America. The closest I come to such distinction is a second cousin who was a runner-up for Ellensburg Rodeo queen.

P.P.S. While our dormant rhododendrons took a beating in the storm, our cabin is intact, and Francis is the talk of Maple Grove Beach. The morning after the storm, all the boats that had been tied to the buoys out front were found down on the rocks past the boat ramp. All except for Francis's! His had moved down the shore a bit, but it was still attached to its buoy. My clever husband used two lines, so even though the lead line broke, the backup line held. Needless to say, he was pleased as punch about that.

January 19, 1963
Los Angeles, Calif.

Dear Mrs. Fortier,

Your jam puts store-bought to shame. As I ate it on a fresh croissant from the French bakery at the Farmers Market down the street from my house, I savored the image you painted with your words. I would love to spend a summer morning in the Pacific Northwest sunshine picking wild blackberries. I also crave your backyard access to crisp apples, plums, and pears, although I am not sure I would trade them for the grapefruit and oranges I pluck from my own trees for breakfast whenever I like.

You are correct. There is a large Mexican community in Los Angeles. Scarcely a century ago, this part of America was another country entirely. It makes for exciting food discoveries. I take Spanish lessons with regular trips to Tijuana and down the Baja peninsula for extra practice in case the borders ever shift again.

My favorite Mexican dish is the tamale, but it is not easy to make, and I suspect you would not be able to find all the ingredients you need up in your Nordic region, especially masa flour, which is a special ground corn. I asked Mr. Rodriguez if his wife has any simple dinner recipes she could recommend. It turns out that he is a widower and did all the cooking for his two daughters when they were growing up. He claims to enjoy it. Imagine that. A man other than James Beard who loves to labor in the kitchen. He suggests carne asada. He is taking me to his local mercado on Saturday to stock a basic Mexican pantry. I will try the recipe first before sending it to you.

In all this talk of food, I nearly forgot my exciting news. I have a job. I am a staff writer for the women's pages at the <u>Los Angeles Herald Examiner</u>. I should explain that after I graduated from Stanford with a degree in sociology, I realized that I had no idea what to do with this achievement. I am hardly the type of person to immerse herself in fieldwork on social conflict or the welfare state. Between you, me, and my electric Royal, it was my own fault. I started as an English major, but the volume of reading turned out to be too much for my eyes. I switched to psychology. Did I last two months in that? Statistics should be listed in the encyclopedia under methods of torture. At this point, in order to be able to graduate on time, I switched once again, to sociology. I wish I'd had a better understanding of the different programs when I started. Thankfully, Mother was supportive. It was important to her that I have the best education and a good job, I think because her life was so difficult after Father died when I was young, struggling to keep our house and raising me on her own. But she also wanted me to find work that made me happy.

Stanford has many paths I could have followed. There is a wonderful Western civilization program, although I am not sure what I would have done with that, either. Education for education's sake does not serve a woman well, as I discovered once I had my diploma in hand. The only work I could find for someone with a dispensable degree and a pair of X chromosomes was teacher or secretary. No matter that I had graduated Phi Beta Kappa.

Out of necessity, I returned to my studies. This time I took a practical course from an enterprising woman named Mrs. Dyer who developed her own method of shorthand. I was able to learn quickly. Within a few months I was a secretary for a Rexall. Yes, it was as dull as it sounds. Fortunately, a friend knew of a program at UCLA that offers a master's degree in journalism in just a year. I always enjoyed writing, and after yet another go at the classroom, here I am at the same newspaper as Aggie Underwood, although she is the city editor with her notorious baseball bat for self-defense, and I am reporting on social club events and writing the odd headline.

I hope I have not bored you with this digression into my misadventures in education. I will close now, but before I do, I would like to address your updated description of me. I must also decline cosmopolitan. I tried stirrup pants recently, but as you know, I do not enjoy looking foolish. I am perfectly happy with my Butterick skirt suits. Mother is an excellent seamstress.

In addition, I have no idea what to do with <u>Sex and the Single Girl</u>. The girls at the paper are chirping with excitement about it. I find it embarrassing. I do not like the presumption that there is only one way for me to be an unmarried, twenty-seven-year-old female. Apparently, I should aspire to something called a "sexth sense," and places where I should make an effort to meet eligible men include Alcoholics Anonymous meetings. As if I have any interest in spending my life drinking Chablis alone.

With warm regards,

Miss Joan Bergstrom

P.S. I agree with you. The existential crisis is one of the worst inventions in modern history.

FROM THE DESK OF MRS. IMOGEN FORTIER

March 13, 1963
Lake Forest Park, Wash.

Dear Miss Bergstrom,

I had hoped to write sooner, but I've been unusually busy with work. I don't have a university diploma, so secretary it is for me! Thank goodness I enjoy my job. As I'm sure you've noticed, I don't write about my life off the island in my column. I work for the Washington State Association of Fire Chiefs. For the past few weeks I've been traveling around the state. I would have preferred to make the trips later in the season when the wildflowers are in full bloom, but the lupine, bluebells, and foxglove I love so much play second fiddle to the importance of meetings about new firefighting techniques.

I'm eager to hear the results of your mercado visit with Mr. Rodriguez. I went to the library for a Spanish dictionary to look up the meaning of the word. I now know that a mercado is a market and carne asada is roasted meat. Did you find the ingredients you needed? Were you able to try the recipe?

Shorey's sent a fine used copy of <u>Italian Food</u>, and I made Mrs. David's risotto alla Milanese. I didn't extract the marrow from the bone myself. I had the butcher do it. Such a velvety combination of flavors with the butter and saffron added. Francis devoured it. This was welcome in and of itself, but his enjoyment of new dishes is the tip of the iceberg. I'm still in a state of astonishment by what happened last Saturday morning.

We spent the weekend at the cabin. Perhaps I should explain that we live in the small town of Lake Forest Park, about an hour from the island and just north of Seattle. Francis is an electrician at the University of Washington, and the commute is comfortable. Anyhow, I had another headache and was resting in bed. I hate to mention my headaches given Francis's migraines, which are infinitely worse. But this particular headache is part of my story so I must include it. I think it's a result of age combined with all the notes I've been typing for work. I made an appointment with an ophthalmologist for next week. I fear it might be time for glasses.

Pardon me for jumping around. Yes, it's my nature, but today I have the added excuse that I'm still giddy. There I was in the cabin on Saturday morning, lying in bed with a cool cloth over my forehead, when I smelled something enticing. I got up, put on my robe, and crept to the kitchen door. I wouldn't have been more surprised to find Sasquatch juggling crab claws. Francis was standing at the stove wearing my periwinkle hostess apron with yellow primroses embroidered on it. He had a Chesterfield in one hand and my spatula in the other. The image is as vivid in my mind as a Matisse. In fact, I have named it: "Husband with Saffron." Oh, Joan, Francis was cooking!

I cleared my throat. He turned around and smiled. I have been married to him for four decades, and I have seen him smile often enough, but this smile was entirely new to me. I wish I had the words to describe it, but my writing talents are with landscapes, not people. I was afraid to speak. I was afraid I would wake up and discover I was dreaming.

I don't know how long we stood there, me staring at Francis and Francis grinning at me. Finally he picked up your saffron and said, "It took me a while to figure out why this tasted so familiar. An infantryman named Chevalier taught me to make an omelette in an abandoned farmhouse in the Somme. Where he found eggs in those lean days, I'll never know." This was the first time Francis had spoken to me about his experience in the Great War. And for him to do so while smiling. I nearly fainted! Then he let out a big laugh and barked, "Sit down, Immy, and stop gaping at me. The food's getting cold."

He served me an omelette glazed with butter, saffron, and herbes de Provence. Herbes de Provence! They came from the Delicacy Shop at Frederick & Nelson. This meant Francis drove all the way into downtown Seattle! This meant he put thought and effort into making this dish for me!

Do I sound silly? A fifty-nine-year-old woman gushing like a callow schoolgirl? My headache didn't vanish but it no longer mattered, and the rest of the day was spent in a pleasant haze as this man I have known since childhood tinkered with his boat winch, as if making me an omelette had been the most natural thing in the world. Who knew that something as simple as a spice could loosen the knots in a man's heart? My apron did not survive, but who cares? I'll be forever grateful for your miraculous gift of Far East saffron.

With warmest wishes,

Imogen

P.S. Congratulations on your new job!

P.P.S. I sympathize with your feelings about <u>Sex and the Single Girl</u>. My friend Hazel read <u>The Feminine Mystique</u> and now all she talks about is society's idealized expectations of women and how the triple-action Hoover is not a substitute for a fulfilling career. This from a woman who once declared her proudest achievements to be her children and her cottage cheese and salmon mold—and not in that order!

June 3, 1963
Los Angeles, Calif.

Dear Imogen,

Saffron as madeleine. I wonder what revived your husband's memory. Was it the taste of the saffron or its scent? And how did the memory return to him? Did it crawl cautiously out of the past, or arrive in one savory burst?

My job is going well enough. Applause, please, for my witty headline about the tent dress, as well as my eloquent contributions to a fascinating article about freezer food trends. I also measure the column inches of the writers in our women's pages. I am becoming an expert with a ruler, putting my master's degree to good use. Do I sound like one of the grumblers we mutually dislike? I hope not. I truly enjoy waking up each morning, putting on hose and lipstick, and driving to Broadway and 11th. Sadly, as of March, my sociable streetcar is gone, victim of the insatiable automobile industry. Otherwise I would zigzag my way downtown from the stop that sat mere steps from the house.

The Herald Examiner building was designed by a lady architect named Julia Morgan. She must have loved Mediterranean castles because the facade is an ornate confection of Spanish, Italian, and Moorish influences. It is so much more pleasurable to cross the hand-painted tile floors of its lobby and share an elevator with energetic newspapermen than it was to pass displays of Listerine and Alka-Seltzer at the Rexall where I nearly surrendered my life. This reminds me. I hope I did not insult you with my thoughtless criticism of secretarial work. Being a secretary is a respectable job, and yours sounds vital to public safety. It is odd to think of you in an office, though, since your columns always paint a picture of you out of doors.

I am happy to announce that my visit to the mercado with Mr. Rodriguez was exitosa. To save you another trip to the library, that means successful in Spanish. The market is located in his neighborhood east of downtown, but I felt as if I had traveled to Mexico for the day. Such an array of tantalizing aromas. He is good friends with the owner, who urged me to shop as if I was stocking up for an end-of-the-world fiesta. I even bought a molcajete, which is a traditional mortar and pestle made of rough stone. Mr. Rodriguez came to the house afterward and taught Mother and me to make carne asada. It is as simple as he promised, but I assure you, it is not like any grilled steak you have had before.

Mr. Rodriguez explained that there are many ways to make this dish. It all depends on where a person is from. In the south of Mexico, oranges are used in the marinade, and in seafront regions a splash of beer is added while the meat is grilling. He suggested we start with a basic recipe (per one pound meat) of 2 tbsp. salad oil, juice of 1 lime, 2 minced garlic cloves, salt, and ground black pepper. You must get your hands on the garlic, since there is no substitute for this recipe.

If you don't have a mortar and pestle, you can mince the garlic to a fine paste with a sharp knife. Whisk it briefly with the lime juice, salad oil, and salt and pepper. Lay out thin cuts of skirt steak in a baking dish and pour half the marinade over the meat. Turn the meat and pour on the other half of the marinade, making sure it's thoroughly coated. Let the meat soak in the refrigerator for at least two hours, and bring it to room temperature before grilling it over hot coals. Carne asada is well-complemented with a salsa, guacamole, and warm tortillas. I told Mr. Rodriguez that tortillas might be elusive for you, not to mention the fresh ingredients for a true salsa and avocados for the guacamole. He recommends ears of corn, grilled and dipped in a blend of lime, butter, and salt. Cayenne pepper, too, if you are up to the heat.

Please let me know how the recipe turns out. I hope
Francis enjoys it and that it leads to new culinary awak-
enings.

With warm regards,

Joan

FROM THE DESK OF MRS. IMOGEN FORTIER

July 9, 1963
Lake Forest Park, Wash.

Dear Joan,

Mr. Rodriguez's carne asada was a rousing success. At first I worried. How would I find enough garlic and limes for twenty or so people? We always host a big gang out at the cabin during the Fourth of July weekend. All of Francis's brothers were coming, Dan, Buck, Hal, and even Rollie driving over the mountains from his ranch in White Swan, plus wives, Francis's sister Irene and husband, cousins Pauline and Ardis, kids, etc. etc. I was an only child, and being part of this enormous family never ceases to thrill me. Where was I? Oh yes, garlic. I remembered that Angelo Pellegrini is an English literature professor at the university where Francis works. Have you read his book? The Unprejudiced Palate. He's a severe critic of American food habits and cultivates an authentic Italian garden at his house in Seattle.

Knowing how much Italians love garlic, I drove to the university and knocked on his office door. Can you believe I was so bold? What a generous man. He gave me a string of garlic and introduced me to an anthropology professor who spent a year in Jamaica. This woman developed an obsession with a dish called jerk chicken, and she has limes shipped from California every summer. She gave me a container of juice from her winter freezer. Neither asked for anything in return. Mr. Pellegrini only wants me to tell him how the carne asada turned out.

I can inform him with all honesty that it was perfection, although I must make a confession to you. We deviated from a wholly Mexican feast by adding heaps of grilled crab from our traps. The crab was delicious dipped in the sauce for the corn. You must try it. My sister-in-law Irene brought a raspberry Jell-O mousse, and there was no way to dissuade Hazel from her cottage cheese and salmon mold.

Francis surprised me once again. He bought Mexican embroidered linens from Trident Imports. The store's owner travels the world to handpick his merchandise, so I'm sure the bright cloths were authentic. After we ate, we cleared the patio and danced to Herb Alpert and Tito Puente. It was such a festive day.

Rest assured that you didn't offend me with your comments about secretarial work. Had other options been available to me, who knows what I might have

become? An aviatrix? A surgeon? Actually, I'm wary of
heights, and I would hate cutting into people, so I suppose the job I have suits me. I may poke fun at Hazel for
her newly adopted views on females and fulfilling ca-
reers, but I'm happy times are changing and a girl your
age is able to choose her own direction in life. In fact, I've
been thinking about your job. Measuring column inches
is hardly worthy of your degree or your talents. You have
a knack for writing recipes. Have you considered asking
your editor if you might write about Mr. Rodriguez's
carne asada? Does the Herald Examiner publish Mexican recipes? It should! I discussed this with Francis on
the drive back from the island, and he agrees with me.

I have been thinking about Francis, too. Of course,
I'm always thinking about him. He's my husband, and
every day I'm doing something for him. Ironing his
shirts or emptying his ashtrays. We have our routines,
bowling on Tuesday nights and playing cribbage on Saturdays after we watch Lawrence Welk. But the thoughts
I'm writing about here have nothing to do with our regular life. They're new to me. I find myself wondering
what's happening inside his head.

I've known him since I was a toddler, we've been
married since 1922, and I've never truly wondered about

his thoughts before. I simply accepted that he doesn't want to talk about the Great War, and I realize I assumed that he fills his head with day-to-day things like electrical circuits at the university or how to make a boat winch out of an old Model T transmission. For the record, the winch works fine now, but he nearly lost a finger assembling it. It gives me a strange feeling, these new musings. Who is this unfamiliar person who has been harboring an omelette recipe among his memories for more than four decades? What other secrets does he carry? I'm looking forward to whatever you suggest I cook next and the revelations it will bring.

With affection,

Imogen

July 31, 1963
Los Angeles, Calif.

Dear Imogen,

Once again you have captivated me with your descriptions. I can imagine you and Francis dancing on your beach to "The Lonely Bull." I told Mr. Rodriguez how happy you were with his recipe, and he was pleased. He says Caucasian people do not appreciate his culture. He talks frankly like that. It is a bit startling, but I like it.

He also says it surprises him how much I love Mexican food. I do not understand this. Why wouldn't I like it? Mother took me to El Carmen for the first time when I was four. This was not long after Father died, back when the cafe was located on the corner of La Brea and 3rd Street just three blocks from the house. Mother has always been curious about food, and I remember that we sat at the counter and ate chile rellenos. What a marvelous dish! During the war we brought our butter ration to the cafe and Senora would keep it in the refrigerator for our tortillas. I can still see her seated at the cash register. She always gave me a sweet when we left, and she and Mother became good friends, so she never made us wait in the line that snaked down the block. One day I met Diego Rivera there. He was impressed by my enthusiasm for hot sauce.

I took your advice and asked my editor if she would let me write an article about carne asada. She was enthusiastic and wants me to include a full menu, so Mr. Rodriguez and I were off to his mercado again, where he knows everyone in the aisles. I have decided to subscribe to <u>La Opinion</u> so I can learn more about Mexican culture in L.A. and also to practice my Spanish, which I should be much better at since I began learning in the first grade before speaking it was discouraged in the schools. So far I have read only one issue. It makes me feel like a foreigner in my own city. I do not mind, though, since I would rather live in a land of enchiladas over meat loaf any day.

I am curious about jerk chicken. I have searched but failed to find a Jamaican restaurant in Los Angeles County. Finally, following my instincts, I went to UCLA. There I tracked down two Jamaican students, both of whom have mothers who, each assured me, make the best jerk chicken on the island. But neither knows the recipe. Could you please ask the professor about it for me? When I promised the students I would try to make it, they looked as if they would melt from gratitude. They are clearly homesick.

It recently struck me how much I have come to treasure our letters. I think about them often as I go about my daily life. When Mr. Rodriguez and I were learning about hot sauces at the El Pato factory, I found my mind straying, eager to share the experience with you. I hope I am not being too forward. What I am trying to say is that I enjoy our correspondence, and I hope you do, too. With affection,

Joan

P.S. In fact, I do know of Mr. Pellegrini. I was ten or so when Mother cut out his recipe for an exotic sauce called pesto from <u>Sunset</u> magazine. She was besotted with it. It inspired her to grow basil in our garden, and we still have it with pasta regularly.

FROM THE DESK OF MRS. IMOGEN FORTIER

August 20, 1963
Lake Forest Park, Wash.

Dear Joan,

Too forward? Not at all. Our letters have become essential to me. Francis even teases me that I grin like a wallflower with a crush on the class president every time the postman brings an envelope with your return address on it.

Mr. Rodriguez sounds like a top-notch culinary guide. You're lucky to have him. My encounters with foreign cuisines are limited. There is a Chinatown in Seattle, and Francis and I meet his brother Dan and wife at the Four Seas there once a month. Francis and Dan claim that their favorite dish on the menu is the old-fashioned. That's a dead horse joke in our pioneer Rat Pack, although it's true we enjoy a stiff drink now and then, and the bartender in the restaurant's Dynasty Room is famous for his generous pour. As for the food, we're fond of the East Dinner, which includes almond chicken and a savory barbecued pork that we dip in hot mustard and sesame seeds.

There's also the thrill of who we might glimpse. Last time we went, our two senators were at the table next to ours talking who knows what politics over pineapple sweet and sour spare-ribs. I've heard that Warren Magnuson has a great interest in China. No wonder he's a regular at the Four Seas. And his legislative partner, Scoop Jackson, was President Kennedy's first choice for a running mate before he settled on Lyndon Johnson because he needed the Southern vote. There's talk they're all working together on civil rights legislation. Imagine having that kind of influence on history. I can scarcely put up the canning every fall, let alone change the world. Such immense responsibility!

Drat and damnation, as Francis's Aunt Cammie would say. Once again I stand guilty of excessive rambling. I don't know how it happens. Senators were nowhere in my thoughts when I sat down to write to you. My intention was to let you know that I accompanied Francis to the university yesterday. My ophthalmologist is there. I had to have my new eyeglass prescription adjusted. The headaches continue. I hope bifocals will do the trick. After my appointment, I was free as a bird until Francis finished work, so I trotted over to the anthropology department to fulfill your request.

Such good fortune. Professor Fox was in her office. What a character! She rhapsodized for more than an hour on the finer points of jerk chicken. Bouncing behind her desk, with her brocade turban and whalebone necklace bobbing along, she asked me, "Did you know that jerk can be traced back to the Taino people who cooked meat over fires made from pimento wood?" It will come as no surprise to you that I replied no, I didn't know that.

She next bounded into a galled description of an argument in certain academic circles about who came up with jerk cooking first. Apparently, there is also a theory that it can be traced back to escaped African slaves known as Maroons. Purists, dear Joan, believe the Maroons learned it from the Tainos. Professor Fox is a purist.

I'm making fun of her when in fact it was a fascinating encounter. Not just her eccentric personality (the turban was turquoise and gold!), but the lesson, too. The word jerk is derived from charqui, which is either Spanish or a Peruvian language called Quechua. It means dried meat. Isn't that interesting? It explains where we get the word jerky. That said, there is also a dispute over the etymology since some experts say jerk might refer to a technique called jerking, or poking indentations in the meat so the marinade is better absorbed. How taxing to be an anthropologist, wading through conflicting versions of history.

With her opinions firmly established, Professor Fox proceeded to inform me that the two essential ingredients in the marinade are allspice berries and Scotch bonnet peppers. I'm not familiar with these peppers, but I'm sure you are. You know so much. Professor Fox has a friend in Jamaica who dries them and sends them to her. If you are in need, she generously offered to spare a few. She insists that this heat is essential. Chicken, though, is not. Pork is also common for this dish, but if you do use chicken, thighs and drumsticks only! (Emphasis provided by the turbaned professor.)

Now for the recipe itself. Along with 1 tbsp. allspice berries and 3 Scotch bonnet peppers, the marinade includes ½ tsp. cinnamon, ½ tsp. cloves, ½ tsp. nutmeg, 1 tbsp. black peppercorns, 1 tbsp. thyme, 1 tsp. salt, 1 tbsp. brown sugar, ¼ cup salad oil, ½ cup soya sauce, and 1 lime. Drat etc. etc. all over again! I also scrawled garlic and ginger in my notes, but didn't write the amounts.

I've never written a recipe so unfamiliar to me before. I apologize for how difficult I must be making your task.

I tried to record as accurately as I could, but Professor Fox spoke at a clip as if she was being chased by hounds. I believe all the ingredients should be fresh, and I realize now that I've left out words like chopped, finely chopped, and ground. There is also some pounding in a mortar and pestle, and crucial whirring in an Osterizer. I hope you can make sense of this. Once you do (I have faith in you), the chicken or pork should marinate for at least 6 hours, but overnight is best.

What a complex job you have. I will never open the food pages of the P-I and take a recipe for granted again. With ever-growing admiration,

Imogen

September 30, 1963
Los Angeles, Calif.

Dear Imogen,

What an entertaining letter. I can assure you that I enjoy your ramblings. They are like sea salt added to a dish, drawing out the natural flavors. As usual, when your letter arrived, I made myself a cup of tea and carried it out to my back garden, where I opened it in the warm autumn sun, in the company of my kaffir lime and curry leaf trees and assorted chili plants. No Scotch bonnet, unfortunately, but I intend to correct that as soon as possible.

Please do not worry about your notes. I enjoy a good culinary puzzle, and you have provided plenty of pieces for me to work with. After a few experimental attempts I felt comfortable enough to invite the Jamaican students from UCLA to the house for a dinner of jerk chicken and my own concoction of rice and beans on the side. Mr. Rodriguez joined us, and with Mother, who is firmly of the British Isles, and I, who am a half-Danish mutt, we were a merry international party. The students were ecstatic to taste flavors from home, and both send hearty thanks.

Mr. Rodriguez enjoyed the dish so much he asked if I will introduce him to more new cuisines. The tables have turned and I am now his guide. Los Angeles is such a varied place. There are foods from dozens of countries at our Grand Central Market alone, and there is a different country in every corner of the city. At the risk of sounding like a shill for the tourism board, Armenia, Italy, Poland, Portugal, India, Greece, you name it and you will certainly find it here. We took a cooking class from Matao Uwate, otherwise known as Mr. Little Tokyo. He is a local celebrity with a popular radio show for the Japanese community.

We learned how to make a teriyaki glaze, and I bought a tempura fryer and a set of porcelain rice dishes in the shape of lotus flowers at a well-stocked shop called Rafu Bussan. Mr. R and Mr. U got on like a house on fire, and Mr. U wants to introduce us to a restaurant called Matsuno Sushi. I am nervous about biting into a hunk of raw fish, but Mr. R says he already crossed that road with ceviche, a popular Mexican dish of raw shrimp, squid, mackerel, and other seafood that "cooks" with lime juice and chili pepper. Given Mr. R's trust in me when it comes to new foods, I feel I must be brave and try it. I promise a full report.

Mr. R and I also attended a rijsttafel table at the Indonesian consulate as guests of my elegant friend Ann Soeleiman, who I met through her cooking class at the Los Angeles International Institute. It turns out Mr. R has an appetite for Indonesian flavors, and he surprised me for my birthday by taking me to a shop he discovered called Hollinda in nearby Temple City. It imports Dutch ceramics and furniture, and the back has a gourmet section with everything we could possibly need to make our own rice buffet, since Indonesia was a Dutch colony in the past. We bought a marinade called ketjap, which is a sweet and tangy molasses-like soy sauce, as well as ground ginger root and ground coconut. Mr. R insists he is going to master Indonesian curry with the dried lemongrass he purchased.

We were so proud of ourselves for our intrepid spirit, we have decided to embark on a culinary adventure once a week. We will take turns choosing, and this week Mr. R chose a bakery called Mrs. Harry's. It is famous for its sweet potato pies. The bakery is located in the Negro part of town. As you can imagine, we looked out of place, but I did not feel unwelcome. This is because of Mr. R, who could befriend a thundercloud with his easy way. We bought a pie at the counter and we were so greedy to try it right away, we took it to a bus bench. I believe I tasted vanilla, cinnamon, and nutmeg mixed into the sweet potatoes, but there was something else, as well, a secret ingredient that has been haunting my kitchen dreams.

Now comes the part of the story that will tickle you. As we were walking back to Mr. R's truck, I caught a whiff of something familiar but unidentifiable in the air. I informed Mr. R that some of my finest food discoveries have involved following my nose, so I followed the savory aroma while he followed me to a restaurant called Claudette's.

Imogen, you will never believe this! The scent was jerk chicken. The menu features mainly Creole food like gumbo and jambalaya, but Claudette's grandmother is from Jamaica. She spent the afternoon teaching us her family's techniques, and even gave me a bag of pimento wood chips to use in my barbecue for authenticity. The world is big, small, and gloriously astonishing all at once! With affection,

Joan

From the Desk of Mrs. Imogen Fortier

October 23, 1963
Lake Forest Park, Wash.

Dear Joan,

First things first. Happy Birthday! A modest gift of our regional delicacy, Aplets & Cotlets, will be arriving in a separate post. They are a confection of apples, apricots, and walnuts, and were quite the hit with visitors last year at the Seattle World's Fair. Next. Happy Anniversary! We've been writing to one another for a year. To celebrate I used the last of the saffron that started our correspondence and made more mussels using your delicious broth. With vermouth, of course, and garlic this time. No substitutes! You're right, it makes all the difference. I hope you don't mind that I mentioned our friendship in my recent column in Northwest Home & Life. I couldn't help myself. I want the world to know how dear you are to me.

While I exchange occasional letters with friends who don't live close, most prefer the telephone ever since Ma Bell started offering inexpensive rates on nights and Sundays. Personally, I don't enjoy the phone. It feels impersonal to me, which might sound strange since a voice in one's ear is a cozy thing. But when I'm on the line, I can mend or play Solitaire, while with a letter I must pay close attention. There is unequaled satisfaction in composing words on a blank page, sealing them in an envelope, writing an address in my own messy hand, adding a stamp, walking it to the mailbox, and raising the flag. It's like preparing a gift, and I feel like I receive one when a letter arrives—yours most of all.

I also hope you don't mind that I've been reading your captivating descriptions of your food excursions with Mr. R aloud to Francis. He thinks they would make a wonderful newspaper column, but I would like to see them in a book. <u>Dining Out with Mr. Rodriguez</u>. Of course, you should probably come up with a wittier title, which I'm positive you could do.

Last week I finally returned to Mr. Pellegrini as promised, to give him my report on carne asada (excelente, according to the Berlitz I borrowed from the library), and to bring him blackberry liqueur to thank him for sharing his garlic and introducing me to Professor Fox. He invited Francis and me to dinner that very evening at their house. I was sure his wife would be furious at the arrival of two impromptu guests, but she behaved as though she had been waiting to greet us since the dawn of time. Perhaps it helped that Mr. Pellegrini is the one who prepared the meal. Between him and your Mr. R, and even my Francis, who knew there were so many men in this world unafraid of spatulas and skillets?

What a meal, Joan! I'm on a friendly basis with freshness. After all, we garden, fish, and hunt, and we pick berries until our fingers turn purple, but every flavor seemed as if it had been given something extra, when in fact Mr. Pellegrini simply encouraged it to be its best self. You should have seen Francis follow him into the herb garden like an eager puppy. When I heard Francis ask how much sage should be used with the pork, I felt the planet tip off its axis. Since when does Francis know sage from a screwdriver?

Over dinner Mrs. Pellegrini pulled the cork from a bottle of vigorous red wine produced by their own hand. It was last year's vintage, while this year's is fermenting in handsome oak barrels in their cellar as I write. They sent us home with a warm loaf of bread, a hunk of parmesan cheese (no grated Kraft in green cardboard for these fine people), and a bottle of wine. We were instructed to enjoy it for lunch, with <u>absolutely nothing else</u>. So much for my tuna fish sandwiches awash in sweet pickle relish and Miracle Whip. As we were getting into the car, Mr. Pellegrini wished us good night and admonished me to never overuse flour in my thickeners.

Once again, food seems to have unlocked a chain around Francis's heart. After his omelette and the fiesta, we had returned to our old routines. But as we were driving home, he asked me, out of the blue, "Immy, have you ever wanted to go to Paris?" I wasn't sure how to respond. I couldn't tell him I never let myself think about such a thing because I knew how painful it would be for him to return to Europe. I have not mentioned this to you before, but I feel I can share it now. Ever since the Great War, Francis has had spells. A kind of darkness tumbles over him, and this is what causes his migraines. In all our years together, I've been careful not to mention anything that might remind him of that part of his life, but in the car, before I had the chance to answer his question, he told me that at the end of the war he had been ordered to assist a group of officers in Paris. He talked about a cafe near Notre-Dame that served a dish called cocoa van, and described how humbling it felt to be a farm boy from Washington State standing in front of the Arc de Triomphe after the armistice. The next night I found a Fodor's Modern Guide to France on my bedside table. And on his? A book called <u>Mastering the Art of French Cooking</u>!

With affection,

Imogen

P.S. Francis hasn't had a migraine since making his omelette.

P.P.S. How was the raw fish?

January 4, 1964
Los Angeles, Calif.

My dear and beloved friend Imogen,

The violent loss of President Kennedy was such a shock. It is only today, for the first time, that I feel I can finally write to you. I apologize for taking so long to send my love and hope that you and Francis are doing as well as can be expected.

My pen falters over the page. What can I write that will not be frivolous at a time like this?

I have been sitting at my desk for an hour now, Imogen. My thoughts are frozen, just as they froze the morning of November 22, when I sat in this very same spot, preparing to write to you. Before I had put a single word on the page, Mother came in and told me the tragic news.

I am sorry for being so grim. The only consolation I find is that people seem to be gentler with one another as we go through this experience together. I suppose everyone feels as fragile as I do, even though we do not talk about it in line at the grocery store. I wonder if this communal tenderness will last, or will it be like after the Second World War, when everyone eventually replaced their memories of gold stars and rationing with automatic dishwashers and two-car garages? I hope not, but at the same time, this sorrow must end. As Mother says, it is disrespectful to President Kennedy to be sad forever. She read <u>A Nation of Immigrants</u>, and to honor him she has started teaching English to Eastern European refugees at the International Institute. I wish I had inherited more of her fortitude.

With much love and lasting tenderness,

Joan

P.S. For some odd reason, my mind keeps circling the same question. Did you ever finish <u>The Seventeen Widows of Sans Souci</u>? What a strange thing to fixate on. Please do not feel the need to answer.

FROM THE DESK OF MRS. IMOGEN FORTIER

February 12, 1964
Lake Forest Park, Wash.

My dear and beloved friend Joan,

Like you, Francis and I are in a deep melancholy. We also wonder if and how our country will recover, although it seems it's already trying. These past few days all people seem to be talking about is the Beatles on Ed Sullivan. I shouldn't judge anybody for this, especially the young. Maybe it's exactly what they need right now, something that looks to the future, even if it is four British boys with odd haircuts.

On our rural island, there is always a neighborly spirit, and it's more generous than ever lately. Even though many around us are stern Republicans, no one's heart can remain unmoved by the photographs in <u>Life</u> magazine of Mrs. Kennedy in her black veil with her children at her side. We are truly grieving as a united nation.

I cannot begin to fathom Mrs. Kennedy's pain when my own body feels as if it is badly bruised. There is not an inch of me that doesn't ache with the magnitude of this loss, and even my new eyeglasses are not enough to fend off headaches I'm sure are caused by my anxieties. After we heard the news, I was terrified the darkness would seize Francis. I have always feared that one day it will overtake him and never let go—but if there is one bright light, it is this: It seems he has finally found his medicine.

When he's not working, he's in the kitchen. We come out to the island on the weekends, the back seat of the Pontiac bursting with groceries and his marked-up Julia Child cookbook. He's determined to become the world's foremost expert on cocoa van, which I now know is spelled coq au vin and means chicken braised with wine. So far, he's concluded that a fireproof casserole produces better flavor than the electric skillet, and his pleasure at lighting the cognac hasn't ebbed.

While he fills our small cabin with the rich scent of bacon lardons browning in butter, I sit in the window and watch our view. We look out onto the deep blue band of the Saratoga Passage, with forests like an old man's stubble on the silhouette of Whidbey Island in the distance. Nature's endurance sustains me, knowing this seascape has been here for centuries and will remain for centuries to come. The white buoys bob in the clear winter light, but not aggressively. Even they seem to know how little motion I can bear right now.

Your mother sounds like a modern-day Eleanor Roosevelt. Another monumental loss. If she were alive now, I'm sure she would offer words of bracing solace. I imagine her reminding me, "You lived through the Great Depression! You led the Sunset Club's charge to equip the day rooms at the Jefferson Park Army Recreation Center during the Second World War. You survived measles! You are not afraid of bears or rattlesnakes! Buck up, Imogen Grace Fortier!"

I'm sitting straighter as I write this. Perhaps I'll find my own refugees to teach. Please thank your mother for the jolt, and I send my debt to you, in perpetuity, for your steadfast friendship.

With much love,

Imogen

P.S. I did read <u>Sans Souci</u>, and I remember enjoying it, but that's all. A thick line separates me from my life during those months before the assassination.

April 16, 1964
Los Angeles, Calif.

Dear Imogen,

Am I a steadfast friend? If that means an honest friend, I am afraid I have failed you. I was deceptive when I last wrote. I told you it took me so long to write because of grief. In fact, the reason was happiness.

Perhaps you noticed in my last letter that I did not mention Mr. R. I could not, you see, because I feared that if I did, the floodgates would open and you would dislike me for being aglow during such a tragic time. Please let me explain before you fling this letter aside and decide I am not the friend you thought I was.

Last fall, on November 21st, after a morning visit to Grand Central Market to buy a Serbian nut roll for Mother's second cousin Inge who was visiting from Oregon, I drove Mr. R back to his house. I had never been there before. Usually, he drives, but his radiator was broken. He lives in a bungalow in Boyle Heights, the old Jewish and Japanese section of the city that is becoming more and more Mexican. Even though winter was on its way, geraniums were in full bloom in bright blue Maxwell House cans on the front porch. He asked if I would like to come in for a cup of coffee. Maxwell House, I assumed.

While I waited in the living room, I noticed a pale green cloth draped over a small lamp table beside the sofa. It was my silk scarf from Bangkok. I had lost it a few weeks earlier. I must have left it in his truck, but instead of returning it to me, Mr. R put it in a place where he would see it every time he walked in his front door. In an instant I was struck by the realization of how often and fondly I thought about him.

If it seems naive for me to have taken so long to discover my feelings for him, please understand. At forty-six he is nearly twenty years older than me. He has two grown daughters and an infant grandson. He is of Mexican descent, which is a wonderful thing to me, but most people are opposed to a mixed match. Surely, you can see why this did not add up to an obvious attraction.

When Mr. R returned from the kitchen and saw me staring at my scarf, he understood that I knew his feelings for me, and I understood that he knew mine for him. He set down the coffee cups and declared that he would like to ride bicycles along the Pacific Ocean with me. I was as delighted as if he had asked me out to the Pacific Dining Car for filet mignon and champagne. We drove straight to Santa Monica, where we rented cruisers and cycled all the way to Malibu. Can you imagine the pair of us soaring up the Coast Highway? With every pump of the pedals I felt like I was pumping bliss through my heart. We stopped for clam chowder at the Sea Lion. Afterward, outside in the brisk ocean air, in full view of the seagulls, Mr. R held my hand. The next day, Mr. Kennedy was shot.

I felt anguish and ecstasy all at once. And such guilt. Who was I to deserve this happiness when a woman like Mrs. Kennedy will never have any with her husband again? I didn't know how to explain to you what was happening to me, but I did more than not mention Mr. R in my letter. I lied when I said the only consolation I could find was that people seemed to be gentler with one another. This was not true.

During those darkest of days following the assassination, Mr. R was my comfort. We bicycled the coast again, and one Sunday we drove to Solvang, a Danish village a few hours north of Los Angeles. We stopped at Ellen's Danish Pancake House for aebleskivers, and Pea Soup Andersen's for pea soup, naturally, as well as two bottles of an excellent California vin rose from their Old Country cellar to take away. We scarcely had time to tour the Santa Ines mission, and it was long after dark by the time we returned to the city.

May I tell you more? I wish I could see your face, to know whether you disapprove. But now that I've started writing about this, I'm a snowball rolling down a hill. I can't stop because every memory I share brings back the full pleasure of the moment. I want to remember each one as many times as possible before my life is through.

By late autumn, wild fennel was dried out all over the city, even in the parking lots downtown. I took Mr. R to one of my favorite spots in Topanga Canyon, and we clipped armfuls of stalks to bring back to my house, where Mother helped us separate the seeds from the pods. The bulb of wild fennel is too stringy to eat, and the pollen can only be collected in the summer. We put the seeds on trays to dry. When they were ready, Mr. R made sausage with ground pork, red pepper flakes, garlic, white wine, and our ground fennel seeds. I added it to a Milanese stew, more white wine along with the rest of the ingredients listed in Italian Food, and we paired it with one of our bottles of excellent vin rose. From harvest to table, I have never had such a perfect meal.

It's a relief to reveal all of this to you. You're my only friend I trust enough to take such a risk. I do hope we are still friends, and that you're not sorry you confided Francis's malady to me. His darkness must be incredibly painful for both of you. It's good to know that he has found a nourishing remedy.

With love and humility,

Joan

P.S. Enclosed is a small token of my devotion.

FROM THE DESK OF MRS. IMOGEN FORTIER

April 26, 1964
Camano Island, Wash.

Dear Joan,

The only thing upsetting to me about your letter is that you think I might disapprove. Rest assured, I will never judge you for following your heart, and we are most definitely still friends.

As for Mr. R being older and Mexican, I'd imagine that an older Mexican man is like any other type of man. Good and kind, or not good and kind, depending on his character. It sounds to me that Mr. R is of the good and kind variety. Please continue sharing stories of your adventures together. They bring me pleasure.

Up here in Washington State, a different kind of relationship flourishes. Francis and Mr. Pellegrini have become friends. Spring is underway, but they are already thinking ahead to winter. At the house in Lake Forest Park they are working on a prototype for a residential greenhouse that can be constructed in an average back yard with minimal fuss with the electrical hookups. Mr. Pellegrini insists that Americans are barbaric to live without fresh herbs year-round. He's in charge of the horticultural aspects of the greenhouse, while Francis is designing a special heating lamp. If I'm to measure by the enthusiasm of their cursing, they're making breakneck progress.

Usually in March and April I'm set to automatic, preparing my beds for the usual corn, tomatoes, green beans, etc. etc. Now, with Mr. Pellegrini in our lives, some measure of brainpower is required. This year I will be planting a hedge of artichokes at his command, with garlic to come in the fall. Despite my love of liverwurst and mustard sandwiches, he insists he will make a good Italian out of me yet.

Joan, I understand your feelings of guilt as your grief and happiness mingle. Spring is such a hopeful time on the island, and despite the pall that continues to hover over our nation, I find it impossible to resist. The air is still chilly as a well-digger's ear first thing in the morning, but as the hours pass it hints at the warmth to come in later months. As the days become longer, the rains change. They are less punishing and more promising, bringing out the native grasses and glimpses of green on the trees. Then there are the little families of deer, grazing as if the entire island is a spring buffet, and wild rabbits are hopping everywhere. As for indoors, do you remember the Fodor's Francis left on my nightstand? The other day it traveled from the bedroom to the coffee table in the living room. When I opened it, I found two Pan Am tickets to Paris! We're going to the City of Light in September!

I was flabbergasted, but all I can get out of Francis is, "When shall we live, if not now?" Apparently, this is a quote from an ancient Roman named Seneca. I can only guess Francis learned it from Mr. Pellegrini, since his own reading tastes run to pocket Westerns. But does it matter? When if not now, indeed! Joan, my life has turned magnificently upside down since your first letter to me. Please write soon, and without restraint.

With unconditional love,

Imogen

P.S. Thank you for the fennel seeds. How should I use them?

P.P.S. Did you ever write your article about Mexican food?

P.P.P.S. Francis mastered coq au vin and has now turned the page to poulets grilles a la diable (more chicken, but this time broiled with mustard, herbs, and bread crumbs).

When he served the latter to Mr. Pellegrini, a three-day argument ensued about the virtues of French versus Italian cuisine. There was even a moment when I feared they might come to blows as Francis defended a fat and flour thickener called roux.

P.P.P.P.S. This is the last one, I promise. Does Mr. R have a first name?

June 5, 1964
Los Angeles, Calif.

Dear Imogen,

Mateo.

That is the first time I have written his name in my own hand. It makes my heart feel as vulnerable as a dandelion in a windstorm. If you don't mind, I will continue to call him Mr. R in our letters. I'm not ready for the intimacy of seeing his name over and over on the page.

For the fennel seeds, you can warm them in honey and drizzle this mixture on sliced pears caramelized in butter. I like to add a hint of Parmesan on top. Not the Kraft you mentioned in a previous letter, but shavings from the authentic kind Mr. Pellegrini introduced you to. How wonderful that he and Francis have become friends. And Paris! You must visit the Musee du Jeu de Paume for me. I have wanted to go ever since I saw Renoir's lyrical "Young Girls at the Piano" in an art book at the library. I begged Mother for piano lessons. I still take them, but I have no natural talent, only enthusiasm and an amateur's mastery of "Goodnight, Irene" and "Greensleeves."

Another use for fennel seeds is Elizabeth David's grilled pork chop. Her original recipe in <u>Italian Food</u>

calls for fennel root and leaves, but I add seeds ground fine in my mortar and pestle to her marinade of olive oil, juniper berries, salt, and pepper. This isn't a nonchalant substitution. It's a preference. There's a distinct difference, in case you are recalling my criticism of ingredient swaps.

Hopefully Mr. Pellegrini will continue to share his garlic until yours arrives next year because you must tuck a whole clove into each pork chop close to the bone. Score the chops not too deep across each side and coat with the marinade. Let them sit for a few hours, turning once or twice, and cook under the broiler for twenty to twenty-five minutes. As Mrs. David writes, the fennel and juniper berries provide "a most original, but not at all violent, flavor."

It's so difficult, keeping Mr. R a secret. It consumes a significant portion of my waking hours. Of course, Mother knows he's my friend, but nothing more. She wouldn't be troubled by his being Mexican, but he's only four years younger than she. When I think about it that way, I can understand why she would be concerned. And I know it would worry her, how people would behave toward us if Mr. R and I made our feelings public. Feelings that I must tell you grow deeper every day.

I wish that once, Mr. R and I could go to El Tepeyac, as we do each Saturday morning, and sit at the counter for our usual breakfast of coffee, eggs and ham, beans, and warm tortillas. While we are eating and talking, the door opens with a jingle, and I look up to see a friend walking in. A friend who knows what Mr. R and I mean to one another. Just once. How wonderful that would be.

With love,

Joan

P.S. The <u>Herald Examiner</u> received many positive letters about my article on Mexican food.

FROM THE DESK OF MRS. IMOGEN FORTIER

July 16, 1964
Camano Island, Wash.

Dear Joan,

This will be a quick note. Summer has us extra busy, with the greenhouse project added to our usual weekday jobs, gardening, and hosting company at the cabin. Crab season has begun, and our niece Kit and her fiance, Michael, come out with their friends every weekend, not to mention Francis's siblings, etc. etc. filling the cabin.

Our crab pots are out front, and Francis has fixed a big metal barrel right on the beach. He lights a good fire to get the water boiling, and after the crabs are cooked, we women sit on the patio shucking until we have a mountain of meat in the middle of the table. We stir up buckets of cocktail sauce from catsup, mayonnaise, Worcestershire, lemon juice, and celery salt, and the kids come running. They eat on their towels on the sand, soaking up as much sun as possible to get them through the next winter. This will go on until late August and I have memorized all the words to "Twist and Shout." Kit brought a portable record player, and Francis ran an extension cord to the patio. The kids play that 45 over and over. It's a catchy song, and I don't mind it too much, although Francis and I tend toward Lawrence Welk.

The other day I realized you don't know what I look like. The enclosed snapshot is of Francis and me at the Sunset Club's Christmas ball. My former sister-in-law was a Sally Brown at Best's Apparel, and she chose the gown for me. At first I resisted the chiffon neckline and beaded overlay. Too much garnish! When I'm not working, I wear pants and Keds like a teenage boy. But Lahoma insisted a woman's wedding dress shouldn't be the only fancy gown she owns during her lifetime.

If you have a spare photo of yourself, please send it to me.

With love,

Imogen

P.S. Congratulations on the success of your article!

July 24, 1964
Los Angeles, Calif.

Dear Imogen,

You look exactly as I have imagined, striking and confident. The dress is elaborate but respectable. Your former sister-in-law has excellent taste. Francis is as handsome as I had guessed he would be, too. A tuxedo hangs well on his slender frame.

I'm enclosing a photograph taken of me at Grand Central Market. Between you and me, I'm fond of it because the lighting makes me look as if I have real cheekbones. Mother did my eye make-up from a picture of Bette Davis in <u>Life</u> magazine.

Mr. R and I are busy and well. I have a bounty of new culinary stories to share with you. When I have a moment to catch my breath, I will write you a long, newsy letter.

Until then, as always, with affection and love,

Joan

PART TWO

Los Angeles, August 1964

"Please extinguish your cigarettes."

The cheerful Western Airlines stewardess pushes a metal trolley down the aisle, eyes scanning for rogue Pall Malls. Imogen hands her tray to the businessman next to her, who gives it to the girl in her trim blue suit. So much more professional than the Alaska Airlines uniforms Imogen saw at the airport in Seattle. God forbid an emergency on those flights. Who on earth could possibly feel reassured by a stewardess dressed like a chic Cossack?

Imogen tilts her head toward the window that's rounded like the screen of a portable television broadcasting the heavens. The movement stirs the sweet fragrance of the orchid pinned to her lapel. A gift with her champagne lunch. Champagne in the clouds at noon!

Why not? This is a weekend of firsts, after all. Flying. Traveling alone. Starry-eyed impulse.

A thrill splinters Imogen's sense of anticipation as she folds her menu and tucks it into her handbag, saving it to show Francis. Now that he's become James Beard in the kitchen, he will want to hear all about the Sirloin de Lesseps in Mushroom Sauce and Italian Swiss Colony champagne. Extra dry, but not too dry, the businessman had informed Imogen, and she nodded as if she too is worldly enough to know about such things. She keeps two Champagne Flight postcards, as well. One to send Francis and one for Hazel, even though she'll arrive back home before the cards do.

Her face warm from alcohol, she gazes across the silver wing. Beneath it, a flat grid of streets sinks into thick, brown smog straight out of a *Tonight Show* joke. She had thought it would feel frightening, looking down at the world like the man in the moon. It's not. None of this is. She thinks back to Francis and his saffron omelette—the unexpected arrival of an entirely new husband after forty years of marriage—and she wonders: Is it possible, at sixty, that she is about to meet *her* hidden self?

This thought intrigues Imogen, and she hopes she'll

be able to explain it to Joan. *Joan*. Imogen laughs out loud and doesn't care at all that the businessman looks at her like she's crazy.

The jet bounces down gently as if the tarmac is her ruffled sea. Imogen follows the businessman, who, like all of the men on the flight, receives a complimentary cigar from one of the stewardesses before entering Terminal 5. The heady smell of jet fuel fills her lungs, and how amazing to think that in a month she'll be on another flight all the way across the Atlantic to Paris. Two flights in a single year, when the farthest she's traveled up to this point in her life is San Francisco, and that by car, for her honeymoon. Now she's seen Mount Rainier from above!

Inside the terminal's waiting area, a family mobs one of Imogen's fellow passengers. A child hops from foot to foot, gripping a sign taped to a yardstick: "Welcome to California, Paula!" There's no one to welcome Imogen. No one knows she's in Los Angeles, except Francis, Hazel, and Mrs. Soderberg at the travel agency. Imogen catches her breath, her throat clenching around fumes of freshly lit cigarettes.

Heels strike the floor, and Zippo lighters snap. A change machine clatters like a pinball parlor. She feels surprisingly sure of herself, on her own in this teeming hall, as she locates the bank of pay phones and strides over to it. She keeps a cautious eye out for pickpockets, as one should in a big city, while fishing in her handbag for her coin purse. She inserts a dime, waits for the tone, then dials the house in Lake Forest Park.

An operator instructs, "Please deposit two dollars and seventy-five cents for the first three minutes."

Her fingers press quarter after quarter into the slot. A long-distance ring follows.

"Hello? Immy? Is that you?"

"Half the women in the airport look like Elizabeth Taylor," she informs Francis.

"If you run into Maverick, make sure to ask for his autograph."

It's Friday, but Francis stayed home from work so Imogen could call and tell him she landed safely. Once she has done this, and promised another call from the hotel before she goes to sleep, she descends underground, into a brightly tiled tunnel that takes her to the baggage reclaim area and then outdoors, where she stares at an alien structure that looks like an umbrella stripped of its fabric. Fleecy white sunlight glints off the hundreds of cars in the parking lots that surround it. The heat is strong and dingy, scrubbing her eyeballs.

As she waits in line for a Yellow Cab, a breezy euphoria electrifies the ends of her nerves. She closes her eyes, holding her face to the August sun until a woman taps her shoulder.

"Your turn." The woman nods at a taxicab.

The sedan glides into heavy freeway traffic, skating over a subterranean city. From the back seat Imogen can just see the tops of buildings nesting low, while palm trees send frayed lifelines past the metal guardrails. A silver Cadillac DeVille convertible cruises by, and she gazes out at the driver, a tanned woman in sunglasses the size of saucers. Imogen is tan, too, but from yard work, not idle living, and when she attempts to fathom such a life, she can't. As downtown approaches, buildings rise out of a brown ribbon, and there is an indistinct outline of a mountain range in the distance, so different from her clear island views.

Getting out of the taxi, Imogen resists the instinct to shield her nose and mouth with a scarf. She doesn't want the doorman at the Mayflower to think she's rude. The hotel is modestly ornate, tall and unusually narrow, with pilgrims adorning one wall of the lobby. Mrs.

Soderberg at the travel agency recommended it over the palatial Biltmore across the street. "It's more personal," she had mentioned in an offhand way that Imogen understood to mean "cheaper." Out of respect, no doubt, for Imogen's mention that she was traveling on a budget.

Imogen can't imagine how grand the Biltmore must be, since her single room here is more than satisfactory, adorned with stately furniture and excessive linens. It's nothing like the motels she stays at when she travels for the fire chiefs' association. On the desk is a copy of the *Los Angeles Times*. She unfolds it. She's tired from travel and daytime champagne. She could stay in, order coffee, savor being in this luxurious hotel room all by herself, and rest up for tomorrow. But one glance at the headlines and no, she's on her feet. She's not about to spend this day of firsts indoors reading about nuclear testing and the Beatles at the Hollywood Bowl.

She stands at the window, gazing out at the sooty haze, and asks herself, "What would Joan do?"

Face freshly washed, Imogen listens while the desk clerk tells her that the library next to the hotel is famous for its rotunda's murals and massive, one-ton bronze chandelier. "Or you might like Grand Central Market. It's a few blocks away."

Imogen pictures the snapshot Joan had included in her last letter. Joan's deep-set Bette Davis eyes and a backdrop of market produce stands. "Is it safe to walk there?" Imogen asks.

The clerk nods. "Until dark."

Imogen sets off up Grand Avenue, using her elbow to clamp her handbag to her side. She's glad she changed into her espadrilles. Despite the flapjack-flat path from the airport, downtown Los Angeles is as hilly as downtown Seattle. When she turns onto 4th Street, following the desk clerk's directions, she tips forward, drawn downhill like driftwood in a current toward the arcades of Grand Central Market.

One step inside the gaping space and her senses burst open. Cantaloupes, grapes, cigarette smoke, roast to go, plums. She can even smell the ice beds cradling shimmering rainbow trout. And the hues of the people! Dark and darker, light and lighter. She's never seen a mosaic like this in Washington, and she forces herself not to goggle at a pretty young woman wearing an emerald green sari.

The aisles resonate with an orchestra of voices, three pounds of tomatoes, a carton of eggs, your best cut of sirloin, please, it's my husband's birthday. Moving with the crowds, Imogen's thoughts whisk back to Pike Place Market in Seattle. When was the last time she had been there? A year ago? Two? The stalls had been abundant, like these, but there hadn't been so many people, what with supermarkets popping up like mushrooms. And it was a crying shame how the new Alaskan Way Viaduct interrupted the sweeping view of Elliott Bay, while Skid Row inched closer, hemming the market with its blue movie theaters and shabby mood.

A dart of uneasiness pierces Imogen's consciousness. Naturally, she'd always skipped the fishmongers' displays of crab and clams. She could get those on the island. But why had she passed by the foreign shops? Pete's Italian Grocery with its imaginatively shaped macaronis, or the spice boutique that advertised imported India Madras curry powder and Spanish saffron.

That's it! That's why saffron had been familiar to Imogen when Joan first wrote to her. Not from a book, but from a sign. A hand-painted sign Imogen retrieved from her memory now. A sign she had passed, more than once, glancing at the words before hurrying on through the lower passageways to hunt for treasures at Goodwill. Joan wouldn't have done that. Joan would have gone inside and sniffed every spice on the shelves before filling her bags with powders to take home and try.

Stepping aside, next to a hillock of ruby red grapefruit the size of bowling balls, she feels a bewildering regret for foods she might have tried, people she might have met. She's read in the *P-I*, there's talk of razing Pike Place Market and replacing it with high-rises. Panic flutters her thoughts. She's never even stepped inside its Turkish restaurant. What *is* a shish kebab, and why has it taken this journey out of state for her to want to try one?

At the stall beside her, pistachios tumble like gravel into a paper bag. Whiffs of wet lettuce and brine hitch a ride on drafts in the air. As she returns to the flow of shoppers, a part of her brain takes a new path, keeping watch for Joan. How funny it would be to spot her. Would Imogen duck and wait for tomorrow, sticking to her plan? Or would she seize the moment? She doesn't know, and since Joan doesn't appear, the question remains unanswered.

Finally, Imogen feels as if she will explode with sight, scent, and sound. She considers everything she has seen. First she purchases roasted coffee beans from as far away as possible, New Guinea, and a small wooden mill as a gift for Francis. She hopes he will find it entertaining to grind his own beans. Next she buys a paste called mole to give to Mr. Pellegrini. The young woman who sells it to her, Miss S. Santos according to her name-tag, explains how to hydrate it and cook it with chicken while Imogen takes careful notes, having learned her lesson with Professor Fox's jerk chicken.

Punchy with a desire to be impractical, Imogen has a vanilla malt for dinner at the market, and back in her hotel room, exhausted, she sprinkles salt on radishes, two bunches for a dime, and eats them for dessert. The Imogen she left behind in Washington never would have dined like this, but the Imogen who came to L.A. on her own would—and does! She changes into her plain Sears nightgown. She writes her Western Airlines Champagne Lunch postcards to Francis and Hazel. Then she calls Francis to tell him she's still safe, and no, she hasn't run into James Garner yet.

Opening the Yellow Pages, she finds the establishment she's looking for. She transfers the address to a sheet of hotel stationery, putting the paper in her hand-bag for tomorrow. She feels wonderfully energized, as if she was on a boat all day. As if her lungs are brimming with fresh sea air, not smog, and her ears ringing with gull song, not car horns. By seven p.m., she is sound asleep.

Eagerness wakes Imogen early. She's grinning, and she can't stop. She orders a light breakfast from room service: black coffee and a dish of cottage cheese and pineapple. She brushes her teeth and tugs a shower cap over her recently waved hair, unable to stop singing "shake it up, baby" while she bathes and puts on the pale green shirtwaist dress she'd carefully chosen. Casual, but not too casual, with a flared skirt because the popular pencil skirts do nothing for her stout legs. She cinches the fabric belt. She slips on her espadrilles again, next best for comfort after her yellow Keds, but she can't wear Keds with her dress. She isn't sixteen, not by a long shot, no matter how invigorated she feels right now. She dabs Avon Honeysuckle perfume stick behind her ears and on her wrists, and softly croons, "twist and shout."

As Imogen hands the taxicab driver the address, her stomach wobbles. The car travels east, away from downtown over a parched cement river. Fever heats the layer of her hidden self beneath her skin. She asks the driver to pass the café and drop her off on the next corner, where she'll have a view and hopefully not be noticed.

Using her flattened hand to shield her eyes from the already sweltering sun, she watches customers enter, mostly Mexican but two older Japanese men, as well. She doesn't know how long she'll have to wait. She's ready to set up camp for the entire morning, but less than half an hour later she sees a dark blue Chevrolet pickup truck pull to the far curb.

The doors open, and Imogen feels light-headed. She watches as the man gets out and walks around the truck to open the door for the woman. The couple approaches El Tepeyac, walking side by side but a foot apart. He's not at all what Imogen expected for a city girl like Joan. No trace of Cesar Romero's flair, not even a suave mustache. He's a bit shorter than average, like

Francis, but where Francis is thin, he's rounder, with a good-natured, clean-shaven face.

Once they have gone inside, Imogen glances at the slender Timex Francis gave her for their anniversary last year. She waits five minutes. She walks toward the café. Her legs are as limp as seaweed. A hammer pounds against her heart. She's never done anything this bold in her life. She grips the door handle, and her sweating hand slides on the metal.

The bell above the door chimes. She steps into air thick with bacon grease and cigarette smoke. The handful of tables are full, and at the counter, in profile, there it is, the face from the photograph. High cheekbones and Bette Davis eyes.

Imogen takes a deep breath, walks to the stool beside Mr. R, and sits down. The woman in profile turns. Sees Imogen. Tips her head, confused.

Imogen watches the mental fine-tuning that causes Joan to blink twice. She smiles.

Joan smiles slowly back. She reaches for the hot sauce next to the salt and pepper shakers. As she draws the bottle back toward her plate of fried eggs and beans, her hand brushes the top of Mr. R's. It's a loose touch, unremarkable, seemingly accidental, but his hand arches up slightly to meet hers, and this—their feelings for one another in a single private gesture—is seen and will be remembered forever by the one friend who knows what Joan and Mr. R mean to one another.

PART THREE

Dear Immy,

I'm still spinning from your visit. Mateo and I talk about it every day, and it never becomes dull for us. It's impossible to express how much it means to me that you've seen him play his violin. I'm so glad you were there when he bought me a cameo necklace from that crusty old Greek in the jewelry district. When one of the girls at work asked me where it came from, I had to mumble a shifty lie about a great-aunt. And of course I can't wear it around Mother. But you know, Immy. You know!

Have you ever met a man as kind as Mateo? Or as . . . I wish there was a word in the English language, or in any language, for how he makes me feel. Safe, but not because of his masculinity. No! I'm not the kind of porcelain female who needs a man to put up his dukes and protect her. It's his character. The world has been tumbling deeper and deeper into the abyss ever since President Kennedy was killed. Those poor freedom fighters in Mississippi, and now the Gulf of Tonkin situation. But when I'm with Mateo, these things don't undo me.

It's strange, too, since I'm aware of much more because of him. He reads newspapers every day. <u>La Opinion</u> and <u>The New York Times</u> because he doesn't trust the local papers, and especially the <u>Los Angeles Times</u>, for the way it portrays Mexicans. He didn't go to college, but he's smarter than any of the men who work at the <u>Herald Examiner</u>. This isn't love talking, Immy. I promise you. It's not just that Mateo has so many facts in his head. It's how he uses them. In ancient times he would have shared a byline on Plato's <u>Republic</u>, I'm sure of it. He's teaching me how to think, although I would never tell him so. How embarrassing to admit that I'm nearly thirty years old with a master's degree and only just learning to flex my gray matter.

I hope Francis enjoyed his coffee grinder, Mr. Pellegrini his mole, and Hazel her medjool dates. I still can't believe we jumped in Mateo's truck on the spur of the moment and drove to the Coachella Valley in the dead heat of August. Please send copies of the photos you snapped of the Joshua trees. I would like to have them to remember our precious time together.

With love, from your beholden friend,

Joan

P.S. I hope you don't mind my mentioning this, but sometimes I marvel that you are a decade older than Mother. I feel as though you and I are sisters. Our natures are connected somehow. I will treasure our midnight conversations, especially about our hidden selves. To think we are made up of so many different layers, and we may never meet all of them before the big sleep. I have been thinking about your comment, about how when we are very young we are so sure of who we are. I admit, there have been times when I longed to be fifteen again, confident that I knew absolutely everything about myself. But I prefer the viewpoint you have been pondering since Francis's encounter with the saffron. The less we cement ourselves to our certainties, the fuller our lives can be. This seems to be something deeper than curiosity or being open to new things. Perhaps if I'd studied psychology I would have the words to describe what I'm trying to say, but I didn't, so I don't, and in any case, this postscript is at risk of becoming its own letter.

P.P.S. You never got around to telling me where you learned to yodel.

From the Desk of Mrs. Imogen Fortier

September 12, 1964
Camano Island, Wash.

Dear Joan,

I'm still spinning, too. Poor Francis. I can't stop babbling about how I drank champagne on a jet plane at noon. <u>And</u> ate sushi. <u>And</u> drove into the desert for dates and watched the sun set over the Salton Sea. What an eerie landscape. It would unsettle me to live out there with those haunting colors every night. Of course, his favorite story is the autograph. You should have seen the look on his face when I told him that I actually met James Garner. I don't think I've ever seen him so impressed. What a coincidence that Mateo built Western sets for the movies before he started his own business. Please thank him again for me. I appreciate the effort he took on my behalf.

It was lovely to meet your mother. What an interesting woman, coming all the way to L.A. from Dubuque on her own to teach schoolchildren. I felt thoroughly uncultured as we walked through the Huntington galleries.

She knows so much about art. And I didn't dare open my mouth when she played her opera records. Don't tell her, but it sounded to me like a box of howling cats. And her cooking! Please send me her recipes for black raspberry dumplings and deviled crab. You come by your kitchen talents honestly.

All the gifts were thoroughly enjoyed. The dates satisfied Hazel's sweet tooth, and Francis grinds a batch of coffee beans every morning, although they have ignited a fresh argument between him and Mr. Pellegrini, who insists there's no finer jolt in the world than Italian espresso and sniffed at trying Francis's aromatic New Guinea beans. Since I have seen Mr. Pellegrini drink plain old Folgers, I'm beginning to understand that the two of them squabble simply for amusement's sake. Mr. Pellegrini did, though, welcome the mole and went to great effort to make sure he prepared it correctly. We all agreed that chicken mole is one of the most addictive dishes we've ever had. Next time you're at Grand Central Market, please tell Miss S. Santos that she has fans up in Washington State.

I must keep this letter short. We're off to Paris in a few weeks, and there's so much to do for an international trip before we go. Traveler's checks, a permanent wave, and another visit to the eye doctor. I promise to send lots of postcards.

With love to you and Mateo,

Immy

P.S. My Aunt Helen was a yodeling champion in her day. I wish I'd inherited her legs instead of her voice, but what can you do?

P.P.S. The world should be ashamed of itself for caring whether you and Mateo love each other. When it comes to its senses (it must come to its senses!), and you feel comfortable out in the open, please visit. Francis and Mateo are sure to hit it off, and we'll take you to the top of the Space Needle. If you come in April, we can tour the tulip fields along the Mt. Vernon Highway, but winter is beautiful, too, with its late-night minus tides. If there's a full moon we can dance in its radiant ivory light.

P.P.P.S. I hope you'll forgive me for sneaking these photos of you and Mateo. I especially like the one where you're looking at the sunset and he's looking at you.

P.P.P.P.S. Although I don't have much to compare them to, I feel confident in stating that tamales are my favorite Mexican food, too!

P.P.P.P.P.S. I wish I could find the ingredients up here for making your delicious quesadillas. (Thank you for teaching me how to spell that!) That way, every time I ate them I would be able to think of the two of us sitting at your kitchen table at midnight, nibbling and drinking Chablis and talking, talking, talking. Those conversations will be forever engraved in my heart.

P.P.P.P.P.P.S. Do you think there is a world's record for postscripts?

September 27, 1964
Paris, France

Ma chère amie Joan,

   Our first meal in Paris. Moules à la marinière. Mussels so brisk and sweet we might have harvested them from the rocky sea ourselves. No saffron, but bread crumbs to bind the broth. Francis is intrigued.

Votre amie dévouée,

Immy

September 30, 1964
Paris, France

Ma chère amie Joan,

The Musée du Jeu de Paume today, and I was thrilled to find this postcard of your "Young Girls at the Piano." The actual painting is enchanting. I studied it an extra-long time on your behalf. I hope you're able to see it for yourself one day.

Votre amie dévouée,

Immy

October 2, 1964
Paris, France

Ma chère amie Joan,

Last night we saw Miles Davis at the Salle Pleyel. Francis is now a jazz fan. We had hoped to see Charles Aznavour, but he's not in Paris so we will have to be satisfied with having watched him on Johnny Carson last spring.

Votre amie dévouée,

Immy

October 3, 1964
Paris, France

Ma chère amie Joan,

Escargot = snail, and I can't, Joan, I just can't. I keep thinking about our slimy Pacific Northwest slugs, and I'm afraid this is where I draw the line.

Votre amie dévouée,

Immy

October 5, 1964
Paris, France

Ma chère amie Joan,

    An entire day at Les Halles. Sacré bleu! I believe the section for the butchers alone is bigger than your market and mine combined. We got lost in the labyrinth more than once, and somehow we've managed to fill half a Samsonite with cheese!

À bientôt, votre amie dévouée,

Immy

FROM THE DESK OF MRS. IMOGEN FORTIER

October 17, 1964
Camano Island, Wash.

Ma chere amie Joan,

(Merci beaucoup to my pocket Berlitz for salutations and "Ou est la fromagerie?" Translation: "Where is the cheese shop?" Who knew there were so many types of cheeses in the world, and with so many pungent odors!)

I can't believe we're already back home in America. Our ten days in Paris feel like the blink of an eye. Or a dream. An elegant, buttery, wine-soaked dream. I'm enclosing a snapshot from the Eiffel Tower. Francis insists the berets were for a lark, but he's been wearing his in the kitchen while he tackles beef bourguignon. And he's switched from Chesterfield to Gauloises. And we don't have a single friend or relative within driving distance who hasn't been corralled into viewing our slides while he narrates—wearing the beret!

You'll be receiving a package soon, and I'm too excited about the culinary delights we smuggled home to let it be a surprise. The saffron (finally, I'm able to return your generosity) is from Morocco, and the baharat spice from Lebanon. France is near so many foreign countries, and the smallest of street markets felt like international fairs. I padded the jars of chestnut spread and Dijon mustard with linen tea towels made by charming nuns near Giverny. I hope everything arrives intact and that you and Mateo enjoy it.

There's so much to catch up on now that we're home. Preparing for winter and more doctors' appointments. The trouble has been narrowed down to my right eye. Thank goodness there's no glaucoma. I'm hoping the specialists will get to the root of the problem soon since the headaches are back. But enough of my ailments. I've been to Paris! I've danced in Paris! I've walked the streets of Paris at three a.m. with mon amour!

Paris, Paris, Paris!

I'm eager to hear how you and Mateo are doing. Write soon, dear Joan.

With love,

Immy

FROM THE DESK OF MRS. IMOGEN FORTIER

October 24, 1964
Camano Island, Wash.

Dear Joan,

I know how busy your life must be. New love is all-consuming. I may be nearing my golden years, but I do remember my youth, and I've read a Mary Burchell novel or two in my time. So please don't feel compelled to write back right away just because I'm sending another letter before you've responded to my last one. The thing is, Joan, when a new experience comes into my life, it doesn't feel real anymore until I've shared it with you, and I have an experience I'm bursting to share and make real.

After a recent doctor's appointment in Seattle, I visited Pike Place Market. First things first, I had a shish kebab at the Turkish restaurant. I'm miserable to think of all the Dick's burgers I've consumed during my trips to the city when I could have been relishing this vibrant lamb dish. God bless the Turks for being so inventive as to mix mint, red onions, and garlic.

But this, my inspiring friend, is merely an appetizer

for the main course of my market adventure. While I was admiring the fall squash, a woman named Alice was taking a survey and asked what the market means to me. I told her my tale of late-blooming appreciation, and she explained she's a member of the newly formed Friends of the Market. This group is determined: The market will never surrender to the wrecking ball!! She informed me that it's happening all around the globe. Even Paris's Les Halles is under threat from the developers. Zut alors! If an institution as ancient and venerable as that is at risk, what chance does a humble Seattle market have when the people who hold the power are declaring it a firetrap and urban blight?

I grew emotional as Alice and I talked. The next thing I knew, I joined the group. Joan, I believe I'm an activist now! I must confess, a decade ago, there were times when I saw students at the university marching with signs protesting nuclear war, and I wanted to join them, but I didn't dare put Francis's job in jeopardy, what with that devil McCarthy and the hysteria about loyalty oaths. Thank goodness electricians weren't under suspicion, so Francis was never asked to sign one.

It turns out Alice is the secretary for Friends of the Market. I offered to help her, which means I'll sit in their office two Saturdays a month to lend a hand with typing, mail, and phone calls. It's already more interesting than it sounds because I'm privy to all sorts of drama. The federal government is offering bundles of money to cities to rebuild their downtowns, and the developers want to roll around in all that dough like Scrooge McDuck. They insist parking garages will revitalize Seattle more than a public market. Sure, the old mare is deteriorating (who doesn't with age?), but our goal is to prove that rehabilitating Pike Place is the key to restoring our city.

I write "our" as if I can take credit for any part of this ambitious idea. I most certainly can't, and that's fine with me. I'm perfectly satisfied with being a worker bee. It's the brainchild of one of our council members, a man with a most enviable name, Wing Luke. He's incredibly energetic. He's an advocate for civil rights, open housing, historic preservation, city agriculture, etc. etc. I mention the latter because this interest is the source of his friendship with none other than our Mr. Pellegrini. Now that we're all connected, Mr. Luke has been out to our house to investigate Francis's greenhouse lamps. What a small world!

A few days ago, Mr. Luke came by the Friends' office to loan me a book. <u>The Death and Life of Great</u>

American Cities by Jane Jacobs. Now, in the evenings, I curl up on the sofa and study urban planning while Francis sautes and deglazes in the kitchen, beret perched on his thinning hair, trying to decide if boiled potatoes or buttered noodles are the best complement for beef bourguignon. Meanwhile, a jazz musician called Thelonious Monk plays on the hi-fi. How strange but marvelous my life has become.

As always, with love and gratitude,

Immy

FROM THE DESK OF MRS. IMOGEN FORTIER

November 7, 1964
Camano Island, Wash.

Dear Joan,

I'm concerned. It's been more than two months since you last wrote. I called your house but didn't get an answer, and when I contacted the <u>Herald Examiner</u> I was told you've taken a leave of absence to Mexico. Please write and let me know you're okay.

With love,

Immy

HOTEL CAESAR
TIJUANA, MEXICO

November 17, 1964
Tijuana, Mexico

Dear Immy,

    Mother forwarded your postcards and letters

HOTEL CAESAR
TIJUANA, MEXICO

November 18, 1964
Tijuana, Mexico

Dear Immy,
    I am so sorry

HOTEL CAESAR
TIJUANA, MEXICO

November 19, 1964
Tijuana, Mexico

Dear Immy,
I do not know how

HOTEL CAESAR
TIJUANA, MEXICO

November 23, 1964
Tijuana, Mexico

Dear Immy,

I enclose each of my false starts so you will know I am being sincere when I say I have wanted to write to you. There is no delicate way to impart what I must confide. I am pregnant and cannot tell Mateo. I have hated keeping this secret from you. You, Immy, my dearest friend, the trusted keeper of my heart. I am a fool. I cannot have this baby. It would be younger than Mateo's grandson. There are ways to take care of it down here. I was given the name of a doctor by a woman who knows about such things. Apparently, there are always women who know about such things. But I have been here for weeks, while the doctor's name remains in the side pocket of my willow green train case and my stomach grows and I can feel

November 25

I had to stop writing. Two days have passed. I am thankful to have an interior room away from the noise of traffic since I sleep most of the time with the curtains drawn.

November 26

Another day has passed.

November 29

The week has passed. What I had been going to write was that I feel the baby moving, but it is so much more than that. When she stirs, what I truly feel is a life of geraniums, violins, cycling the coast, and Mateo's child that I want so desperately but know I cannot have.

November 30

And another day. I will send this letter as it is because I do not know how to write anything more coherent.

With hope of redemption,

Joan

HOTEL CAESAR
TIJUANA, MEXICO

December 1, 1964
Tijuana, Mexico

Dear Immy,

Am I going crazy? Immy, this morning I woke up late and kissed my sleeping husband on the forehead. I know the bed was empty, and I know I don't have a husband, but I swear to you, I gazed at Mateo's closed eyes, his dark lashes, his soft brown cheek resting on the pillow. I eased out of bed so I wouldn't wake the man who wasn't there, and I showered and then got properly dressed for the first time in weeks.

Outside, the heat was already blazing, and the chewing gum boys were hard at work, although as soon as any of them discovered that I speak Spanish, they lost interest. I walked down Avenida Revolucion exploring the arcades. I encountered shopkeepers I knew from past years' visits, and I told them I was going to have a baby. I hadn't realized how desperate I was to say it out loud. To have someone hear me say it. I was ravenous for them to make a fuss and congratulate me. I couldn't get enough, explaining how my husband and I are hoping for a girl, and we intend to name her Frida. I did not mention that we chose this in honor of the storm that brought your first letter to me, or that we decided on the Mexican rather than German spelling given to the name of that storm.

One woman gave me a piggy bank, except it wasn't a pig but a darling ceramic burro, and another sold me a hand-embroidered christening gown for one-tenth its value. I bought a handsome leather belt for Mateo, and a deep clay cazuela to make feasts for our families who will never meet. I carried my flight of fancy in a large raffia bag embroidered with fuchsia flowers, walking and walking, Frida and I in a loose ribboned smock, until I came upon a crowd gathered around a cart next to a car wash.

The air was thick with the smoke of charred meat. It struck me that I had eaten little other than beans and rice with tortillas in weeks. Poor Frida. She must have been swimming around in my belly starving for flavor. I ordered the only dish the cart sells, a carne asada torta. Between the marinade, pickled onions, mesquite mixed in with the coals, and my hunger, I have never tasted a dish so gratifying. I bought one to take to Mateo, but as I returned to the hotel, I remembered that he was not there. He does not know I am in Mexico. He does not know about Frida.

I had to sit down in the nearest cafe so I wouldn't faint from sadness. There was only Nescafe on the menu, but the waitress was kindhearted and made me a traditional Mexican coffee with cinnamon and piloncillo that one usually finds in rural towns. I drank it quickly, not only to revive myself, but because Frida loves caffeine. It wakes her instantly, and I wanted to feel her dancing.

I watched the tourists passing by, young women my age in pedal pushers and newly purchased huaraches. I wondered which of them has the name of a doctor hidden in the side pocket of her train case. Which of them walks the city pretending that a husband she does not have is waiting for her back at the hotel? Which of them has already named a baby she is not going to keep?

Your delusional friend,

Joan

HOTEL CAESAR
TIJUANA, MEXICO

December 2, 1964
Tijuana, Mexico

Dear Immy,

I am better today, if better means not conjuring marital apparitions in my hotel room.
With love,
Joan

FROM THE DESK OF MRS. IMOGEN FORTIER

December 12, 1964
Camano Island, Wash.

Dear Joan,

You aren't going crazy, my dear friend, and rest assured, your struggles are safe with me. I can't imagine there are any words that will bring you the kind of comfort you need right now, but I must try, clumsy as my efforts might be. I've decided I will give you a secret in trade for the one you have given me. To distract you, if such a thing is possible, and so that you will never feel unequal in our friendship because I know more of your heart than you know of mine.

I don't know the first moment I realized I was in love with Francis, but I can't remember a time when I wasn't. As a child I was his shadow, but when he left for the Great War, I was a fourteen-year-old tomboy with a pudgy nose, and he was engaged to a popular girl named Violet. He would have spent his life devoted to her if not for his older brother Rollie. At the end of the war, Rollie received the Distinguished Service Cross for extraordinary heroism. I can never get the details right, so I will quote directly from the newspaper article:

> "Sergeant Ralph Fortier, Headquarters Company, 361st infantry (No. 2256264). For extraordinary heroism in action near Gesnes, France, September 26, 1918. Sergeant Fortier, who was in charge of the signal section attached to the attacking battalion, displayed remarkable coolness and disregard for personal danger in bringing the battalion telephone line through heavy artillery and machine gun fire to the ridge which was being attacked, and there establishing communication with regimental headquarters."

When Violet learned of this, she dropped Francis like a hot potato and set her sights on Rollie. They were married a year after his return from Europe. Francis wasn't at the wedding. He was away recuperating from a mysterious injury no one talked about. Even though I was only seventeen, once he came back to Toppenish I could see signs of the darkness that had infiltrated every cell of his being on the battlefield. I hadn't heard of shell shock back then, and even now I cringe to write it on this page.

Too many people still associate it with lack of moral fiber, and I can't bear anyone thinking that of Francis, but I trust you to know better.

One night after Francis returned, there was a party, and he had too much bootleg whiskey. His sister sent me to check on him, and I found him out in the barn. He was thoroughly soused, and he told me how ashamed he felt. It wasn't just the darkness, Joan, or being jilted. He and Rollie were too dear to one another, and he got over that quickly. Francis had a secret no one but his doctor knew. I hope it's not indecent of me to share this with you. Francis is impotent. A doctor prescribed potassium bromide tablets for his mental condition. While it calmed him, it also had side effects that should not have been permanent but were.

We were sitting in the hayloft overlooking the alfalfa fields when he confessed this. Whenever I smell freshly cut hay, I think of that night. It's the night my life changed its course. I'm sure it was a combination of his drunkenness and my innocence that gave me courage, but I informed him that he could propose to me if he liked. I wanted to be his wife. I had wanted it long before I knew what that kind of love means, but there was more to it. I wanted Francis to keep on living. I don't think he would have taken his own life, but I do think he would have disappeared into his darkness and become one of those men you see on park benches, eyes blank as slate, stuck inside a war that doesn't end.

Another thing you must know. While I have not for one second regretted my decision to marry Francis, I also understand what it's like to want a child with your whole heart. There was a period when I was around your age that I would carry a warm loaf of bread wrapped in a dish cloth around the house like an infant while Francis was at work. Those were painful times, but that particular longing was only one small part of the much bigger life I have shared with Francis.

Our marriage has been satisfying and amiable. Ordinary words, I know, but an ordinary life suited me. Then you came along and uncovered the layers neither of us could have imagined existed. Francis is alive in ways I never dreamed of on our wedding day. Our marriage is alive in ways I never dreamed of.

I'm sure it feels impossible to believe now, Joan, but your life is going to take turns you can't begin to anticipate. Perhaps tomorrow, or perhaps when you reach my ripe old age, it will deliver unforeseen joys that will lift your spirits to the heavens. I can make this promise to you because you taught me that it's true.

Whatever you decide to do, you have my full support. If you choose to let Frida go, I'm here for you, and if you choose to keep her, I will be her proud and doting Aunt Immy.

With love,

Immy

P.S. I bought the Frangos for you (arriving by separate post) before I received your letters. I know chocolate won't make things better, but it certainly can't hurt. I'm also sending the latest Helen MacInnes for distraction.

January 3, 1965
Los Angeles, Calif.

Dear Immy,

I am humbled that you trust me with such an intimate story, and it is certainly not indecent to share such a thing between friends as faithful as you and I.

I am back in Los Angeles. I decided that it would be cruel to deprive a child of a loving Aunt Immy, so Frida will stay. I am not sure what to do next. I cannot return to my job at the <u>Herald Examiner</u> in my condition, and whenever the phone rings, I make Mother answer it and tell Mateo I am still in Mexico. Mother being Mother, she took the news with her typical aplomb, exhibiting an absence of shock and heaps of gumption. First things first, a gold band to wear on my ring finger. Then an obstetrician in Beverly Hills who specializes in unwed Hollywood starlets and discretion.

Please write back soon and tell me about the latest argument between Francis and Mr. Pellegrini. Tell me how you are saving your Seattle market. Fill the corners of my mind so there can be nowhere for doubt to lurk.

Happy new year, and with love always,

Joan

P.S. Thank you for the thoughtful gifts from Paris. Frida loves the chestnut spread. I mixed it with whipped cream and folded it into crepes with a dusting of orange zest on top. I took no more than two bites before she started wriggling with delight in my womb.

P.P.S. I am a self-centered friend. I have not asked about your headaches. Have the doctors cured you? I hope so. I hate the thought of you in pain.

From the Desk of Mrs. Imogen Fortier

January 14, 1965
Lake Forest Park, Wash.

Dear Joan,

When I learned that Frida will be joining us in this world, I wept with gladness. You may be filled with uncertainty, but I'm not. Frida will be the first female to summit Mt. Everest! The first female brigadier general! The first female on the Supreme Court! And of course the first female to storm the White House!

Unfortunately for entertaining stories, Francis and Mr. Pellegrini have been unusually subdued as they experiment in their greenhouse these days. Francis continues with his culinary exploits, and I'm sure he'll have fulfilled the "mastering" part of Mastering the Art of French Cooking by summertime.

As for my meager contribution to saving the market, it involves my finely honed shorthand skills and taking dictation while Mr. Luke and his colleagues heatedly combat the Central Association's plan to replace Pike Place with terraced garages and high-rise offices and apartments. The association is made up of gloomy downtown businessmen who continually blame the suburbs for their dwindling clientele. They produced their plan because they can use it to rake in federal funds to do a formal study. The plan is filled with equally gloomy sketches of Soviet-looking towers they insist will improve the city, never mentioning all of the people who will be displaced.

Where will they go? It's about more than not being able to afford the new apartments. Oh, Joan, I'm learning such terrible things about where people who don't look like me aren't allowed to live. It's startling, how much I've not been aware of. But over the years I've also learned better than to wish I could change my past. Instead, I will meet myself where I am—becoming enlightened alongside the radicals, artists, and Italians who own shops in Pike Place and sit in our office for hours on end drinking coffee and declaring that a marketplace by and for the people is essential for the health of a civilized society. Apparently, I'm discovering, Communist architecture is acceptable to the association, but Communist attitudes are not! (This is a joke. There's no question about which side of the Cold War I'm on, although between you and me, I don't see what's so detrimental about sharing.)

As Mr. Luke and his friend Victor Steinbrueck, who is an architect, produce counter-plans, I type them in triplicate and mail them to the appropriate people. I pause at lunchtime for kebabs, and during one of my lunch breaks, I was enlisted to help type invitations for Art Stall Gallery, a cooperative that is opening next month and is owned by women artists.

It's invigorating, the kinship that fills Pike Place Market. Even if a market is part of the new plan, it won't be the same. The shops will be slick, and there certainly won't be any homey kebab cafes. The Central Association is arguing that Pike Place is a potential hazard to health and welfare, but honestly, Joan, they just want to prove it's hit the skids so they can get the fed's money and make more money. Other neighborhoods in Seattle need real help, but other neighborhoods don't have our views of Elliott Bay and the Olympic Mountain Range, marred as they are by the freeway, but exquisite nonetheless. Real estate development, I'm learning, is mostly about greed. Apparently, Francis has known this all along. He laughs at my naivete, but Mr. Luke says I bring refreshing energy to our meetings.

Last week I met with a specialist who took X-rays of

my eyes. As soon as I know the results, I will share them with you.

I wish this letter was more entertaining. Apologies for boring you with a lecture on the dark underbelly of urban renewal, but there is not much else to tell besides my bowling scores. Not bad, 141-124-156. Winter is never an exciting time up north. The deciduous trees are bare, and the evergreens grow dark and gloomy under gray skies. We did have a little snow last weekend, and Francis and I were able to sled the hill behind the cabin.

With love,

Aunt Immy (It has a lovely ring to it, doesn't it?)

P.S. I've asked Hazel to teach me to knit so I can make Frida more snuggly booties than she will ever need in California, giving you all the more reason to bring her up here so she will have an opportunity to wear them.

February 7, 1965
Los Angeles, Calif.

Dear Frida's Aunt Immy,

Thank you for taking my mind off my situation. I did not find your letter boring at all. I'm enclosing a check for $10 written out to Friends of the Pike Place Market. I hope that is correct. It is not much, but I want to support your cause.

My life is moving forward. Mateo has stopped calling the house, and there has been a turn with my job. I received a call from Jeanne Voltz. She is the editor of the food pages at the <u>Los Angeles Times</u>. She told me she was a fan of my article about Mexican food for the <u>Herald Examiner</u>. She is looking for part-time help and asked if I would be interested in writing about ethnic food for her. You might remember me telling you how Mateo feels about the <u>Times</u>. Am I being too idealistic in thinking that maybe I can change some attitudes with Mexican recipes? Is it wrong of me to let Jeanne assume I am married?

In any case, it is a relief to have work to focus on, because left to my own devices, I am afraid of returning to the near madness I barely escaped in Tijuana. The other day I did something that I know was very foolish. I visited the Bailey Memorial Home and Hospital pretending I was researching an article. At the time I was simply possessed to go there, but in hindsight I realize that I wanted to know what Frida is in for.

I am pregnant like the girls there, but the ring that Mother bought for me made all the difference. The matron spoke right in front of the poor girls about how they are a social problem and a symptom of an infected society. I remember whispers about "bad girls" when I was growing up, but none of these girls looked bad. They just seemed sad, tired, and too young for the burden they carried. The matron introduced me to a case worker who insisted on the importance of handicraft and gripe sessions. The case worker has a psychology degree, and she explained that girls get pregnant out of wedlock because of their childhoods. Is this true? Am I in my condition because of my father's death when I was young?

The matron would not let me speak to any of the girls alone, but as I was coming out of the washroom, one pretty teen hurried up and told me how the guests, as the matron calls them, are not addressed by name when visitors are not around. Each one is given a number, as if they are inmates in a prison. She was crying, and she clutched my hand and asked me, would I please say her name? Susan. That was all she wanted. Immy, it was awful. Like the rest of the girls in the home, Susan will give her baby away for adoption. The matron did not use such an ugly word as bastard, but she made it clear that the offspring of an unwed mother has only one disreputable destiny. Frida is going to be a mixed-race child without a father. Will her life be better if I give her up?

I am certain you must be wondering why I refuse to tell Mateo about Frida. If I did, he would marry me. He is an honorable man. But this would surely hurt the daughters he already has. His family does not deserve the pain and shame this would bring.

With love,

Joan

P.S. I am enclosing the small packet of Peruvian peppercorns I had meant to send to you for Christmas. In winter the pepper trees here grow heavy and rattle in the arid winds, and I always gather and dry a batch. If you do not have a grinder, you can crush them in your mortar and pestle. Use sparingly. Their flavor is distinct.

P.P.S. I almost forgot to tell you. The woman who wrote the French cookbook Francis is so committed to is on television here in Los Angeles. Last fall the city got a new educational channel, KCET, and its schedule includes a program called <u>The French Chef</u>. It is unlike anything I have seen before, approachable and even funny. Julia Child has the most unusual voice, and although she studied at the Cordon Bleu, it turns out she was homegrown right here in Pasadena. Has the program come to your area? I hope so for Francis's sake.

P.P.P.S. I have discovered the suspense novels of Phyllis A. Whitney. I highly recommend her for escape.

P.P.P.P.S. Frida is due on June 20.

From the Desk of Mrs. Imogen Fortier

February 21, 1965
Camano Island, Wash.

Dear Joan,

<u>Do not</u> give Frida away! She needs you to teach her about saffron, jerk chicken, and carne asada.

I have taken your advice and checked out three novels by Mrs. Whitney from the library. I am now the one in great need of distraction. You have so much on your mind, and I don't want to add to your worries, but you and I can't keep secrets from one another, so I'll write this quickly and get it over with. A tumor is pressing against my right eye. The doctors are trying to decide between surgery and radiation, but either way, they feel the eye must go. Francis assures me I will look dashing with a pirate patch.

It's your turn now to tell entertaining stories to keep my mind from filling with fear.

With love,

Immy

P.S. Unfortunately, our educational KCTS is stuck on driver's education, calculus, and an abundance of university science courses. There hasn't been a single sighting of <u>The French Chef</u>. Perhaps I can use this to entice Francis into a trip to Los Angeles with me.

March 1, 1965
Los Angeles, Calif.

Dear Immy,

Your news has stunned me, but I will not be morbid. Aunt Immy shall live a long and healthy life, and Frida will be the only girl in her class with a pirate for a godmother. You will be her godmother, won't you?

I have news that will serve as a good diversion for both of us. It turns out that Jeanne Voltz, my new boss I mentioned, is a real newspaper woman. She believes the food section should be about more than just putting three square meals on a table and women's club potlucks. She is interested in how changes in the food industry are affecting our society, and natural foods and nutrition are extremely important to her. She takes me back to what I learned at UCLA about the principles of responsible journalism. In a different world I am sure she would run the <u>Times</u>. For now, though, she capably defends her domain, which generates more advertising than any other section, and demands excellence from her writers.

It is exciting to be challenged, Immy. When I realized

the kind of woman Jeanne is, I gathered my courage and asked her if she would be interested in a weekly column about Mexican food. She applauded the idea but informed me that her readers' needs are her priority. To gauge their interest, she posted this notice on the back page of the food section.

Send recipes, requests, and information about
Mexican food to Joan Bergstrom,
Food Department, Los Angeles Times,
Times Mirror Square, Los Angeles, 90053.

By the end of the following week I had received more than a hundred letters! People asked about jalapeno jelly and tequila, and they wanted to know how to adapt Mexican flavors to "Yankee tastes." My new column will be called "Borderlands." Jeanne has even hinted that she might have me travel and bring back regional recipes from Mexico.

You cannot imagine how thrilled I am to have a column of my own to exchange with you. I doubt I can ever meet the high bar you have set with "Letter from the Island," but I promise I will do my very best to try.

As for the rest of my life, my feet are so swollen they look like two hams, and I am sound asleep by eight every night.

Your tired friend,

Joan

FROM THE DESK OF MRS. IMOGEN FORTIER

March 28, 1965
Camano Island, Wash.

Dear Joan,

I accept my appointment with a pledge to be the best one-eyed godmother in the history of godmothers.

Congratulations on your new column. I'm certain you will enrich many lives in the way you have Francis's and mine. I hope it's not too much to ask you to cut out "Borderlands" and include it with your letters.

The decision has been made. There is going to be a surgery next week to remove the tumor.

I don't want to burden Francis when I see the great effort it takes for him to be strong for me, but I know I can share my deepest feelings with you. I'm terrified of being put under anesthesia and having a knife cut into my eye. I'm terrified the surgery won't be a success and I'll still need radiotherapy. I made the mistake of reading an article in Reader's Digest about cancer treatments. I thought it would steady my nerves, but did you know, radiotherapy is dicey business when it's administered

near the brain. Last I heard, my eye is definitely near my
brain. I'm worn out, Joan. Please bear with me.

With love,

Immy

April 5, 1965
Los Angeles, Calif.

Dear Immy,

My precious friend, I wish I could dissolve your fears. I am certain your surgeon is the best. Francis would allow nothing less. Please get lots of rest with the knowledge that your recovery will be filled with saffron omelettes and all sorts of magnificent creations from the loving culinary genius of your devoted husband. As for me, I promise to send only the most amusing of stories.

With all my love,

Joan

P.S. Enclosed is my first column. I consider myself a journeyman writer, but I do hope I have made you proud.

BORDERLANDS

The Flavor of Mexico

BY JOAN BERGSTROM

TIMES STAFF WRITER

If you are what you eat, as some people say, then everyone in Los Angeles is partly Mexican. Here, Mexican food is as basic as the hamburger. It is eaten in restaurants, at taco stands, or at home, where it can be prepared from scratch, taken out of a can, or thawed from a frozen dinner.

This obsession is to be expected when you consider that California was part of Spain and then Mexico until it was taken by the United States with the Treaty of Guadalupe Hidalgo in 1848. Even today, Los Angeles can claim one of the largest communities of Mexican people outside of Mexico City.

We live surrounded by traces of Mexico—customs, place names, and people of Mexican origin. The patio, a California institution, came from Mexico and so did the barbecue (barbacoa). On occasion, I have had to speak Spanish in order to make a purchase. And in some restaurants I have heard nothing but the soft ripple of the Spanish language.

Those who want to prepare the food themselves will find the city rich in the ingredients for Mexican dishes. There is scarcely a food item that you can't buy, from epazote, chorizo, and queso fresco to the unslaked lime and dried corn required for making tortillas.

Mexican cookery to me is the most exciting in the world—intricate, colorful, and varied. If I could only eat one type of food, I would be happy to confine myself to that of Mexico. The following is a favorite recipe to launch this column. It is one that I prepare often at home, and it makes a perfect late-night snack for long conversations with a dear friend.

=====

QUESADILLAS AVENIDA RUIZ

These quesadillas that I found in a neat little café on Avenida Ruiz in Ensenada are as tasty as they are simple to make. A clerk in a Tijuana market prescribed the Chester cheese, which has a mild cheddar flavor and the advantage of softening but not running. Good substitutes are medium Tillamook, mild cheddar, or Monterey Jack cheese.

2–4 tbsp. lard
8 corn tortillas
8 slices Chester cheese
8 strips green chile
1 onion
crumbled cheese

Melt the lard in a skillet. Place a tortilla in the lard and on one half of the tortilla set a slice of cheese and a strip of chile. When the tortilla has softened, fold the other half on top of the filling and press down. Continue to fry on both sides until the doubled tortilla is lightly browned. Remove, pat with a paper towel, and keep warm until all the quesadillas are cooked. Serve them topped with rings of onion sliced paper-thin and sprinkled with a crumbly cheese such as Mexican queso enchilado or queso de Sonora. Makes 4 servings.

FROM THE DESK OF MRS. IMOGEN FORTIER

April 10, 1965
Lake Forest Park, Wash.

Dear Miss Bergstrom,

Immy's surgery was a ~~sucess~~ success. She is now re-
covering and ~~wik~~ will not be able to use her typewriter for
a ~~wn~~ while, but she asks that you please keep writing to
her. I will read your ~~ler~~ letters aloud if that is all ~~rigght~~
right with you. She also wants me to tell you she read your
first column before her surgery. She thinks it is ~~aaa~~ genuine piece, and she was so bursting with pride she ~~asjed~~
asked me to go to our ~~statinery~~ stationery store and have
Xerox copies ~~nade~~ made for all of her ~~nursdes~~ nurses and
the members of our bowling league.
With warm regards,
Francis Fortier

P.S. Apologies for so many ~~mia~~ mistakes. For all of my
skills as an ~~electt~~ electrician, I have ~~alays~~ always had ten
thumbs when it comes to the typewriter.

P.P.S. Immy has asked me to ~~addd~~ add her exuberant approval of the ~~reciope~~ recipe you chose. She was glad to be ~~remminded~~ reminded ~~off~~ of your wee ~~jour~~ hour heart-to-hearts in L.A.

April 15, 1965
Los Angeles, Calif.

Dear Immy (or do I address this to Francis?),

I admit I am having difficulty writing this letter. My euphoria at your triumph over the scalpel makes me so dizzy I can scarcely see straight. In addition, I feel somewhat shy about writing to you through Francis. Francis, I hope you don't take offense, but the thought of your reading aloud the story I am going to share gives me pause. Forgive me if you find parts of it too female, but censoring myself in any way will detract from the amusement I hope to provide. Amusing you (Immy) is my sole objective.

Today's installment of Aunt Immy's Recovery Room Entertainment comes straight out of Lord Byron's "stranger than fiction" department. You will never believe who I was asked to interview for the <u>Times</u>' Sunday magazine. Helen Gurley Brown. THE Helen Gurley Brown of <u>Sex and the Single Girl</u> fame. The very same Mrs. Brown whose dating suggestions I groaned about in one of my first letters to you. She is on tour for her new book, <u>Sex and the Office</u>, and I was charged with talking to her about the ancillary industry her books have

spawned: cookbooks for trapping a man. <u>Saucepans &</u>
<u>the Single Girl</u> is just one of a steady supply that publish-
ers have in the works. Jeanne would never have assigned
this article, but I was specifically requested by a senior
male editor at the magazine. Why me, big as a house in
my maternity kaftan and ham hock feet? Why not one of
the young female reporters in their modern Jax fashions?
I have no idea.

I felt like an elephant thundering into Chasen's, as
unlike Mrs. Brown as could be. She arrived in a delicate
cloud of Arpege, wearing a form-fitting, zebra-stripe
dress cut well above the knee. She is a tiny woman, thin
and taut as a stick of uncooked spaghetti. My stomach
for two was set on the grenadine of beef and potatoes
hashed with cream. Fortunately, Mrs. Brown ordered
first and kept me from the faux pas of this boorish choice.
I followed her lead, a paltry heart of palm salad with vin-
aigrette, and a Perrier, which she drank through a straw.
Needless to say, Frida and I were starving throughout
the interview.

I was awfully nervous to meet Mrs. Brown. It is irra-
tional, I know, but I was afraid she would sense the criticism I once expressed to you. I feel badly now that I have
met her. From the start she was friendly and got straight

down to business. This put me at ease, thankfully, since I was also feeling inadequate because her press agent informed me that she had spent the morning with a journalist from The Saturday Evening Post, a clever young woman named Joan Didion who made a splash a few years ago with an essay in Vogue about self-respect.

I only know about the essay because I was assigned to write the headline for a feature article in the women's section of the Herald Examiner about collegiate fashions to boost a girl's regard for herself. The article quoted lines from Miss Didion's essay. I still remember one of them: "The charms that work on others count for nothing in that devastatingly well-lit back alley where one keeps assignations with oneself." I thought at the time, and I suppose I still do, that some women are simply more complex than I will ever be. To top this off, Mrs. Brown was going straight from her conversation with me to taping the Johnny Carson show.

So there I was, wedged into her busy day between these two notables, with George Peppard sitting in the next booth over. Mrs. Brown and I chatted about yogurt, soy-date muffins, Triscuits versus Ry-Krisp, and why food should be a priority for single women. There is an entire chapter in her new book about preparing one's own brown bag lunch for the office. Here is an example: canned shrimp with cocktail sauce, half an avocado, a hard-boiled egg, and Saratoga flakes for crunch. Plus wine brought in a Thermos and drunk from a china cup just in case alcohol at work is frowned upon.

I thought we would be discussing all of this in the context of seduction, but it turns out Mrs. Brown is an advocate for financial independence. Making one's own lunch for work, no matter if the ingredients are as glamorous as smoked salmon and Camembert cheese, is a matter of saving money for better things, like holidays in Bermuda. Mrs. Brown brings lettuce to her office in a wax paper bag and chops her own salad right at her desk. Although she did not say so directly, I believe her purpose with her books and her magazine is for women to be in control of their lives, and it just so happens that this philosophy is more palatable under the provocative cover of sex.

I really liked her, Immy. She was not at all what I expected. She was very executive and not the least bit arrogant. At one point she even asked me what dreams I have for my life. She worries about what happens to a woman's dreams once they are married and have children. (I beg your pardon, Francis, for mentioning this, but I did not correct her about the marriage part, even though I am sure she would not have judged me.) I told her about my column. She asked if it makes me happy. I said I enjoy it, but happy? Somehow, I ended up confessing that what I really want is to write a cookbook about how California food is influenced by so many different international cuisines. The next thing I knew, she was giving me the name of her literary agent in New York. Henrietta Neatrour. Isn't that chic? Mrs. Brown gave me permission to say that she recommends me.

I hope my story has not been too frivolous, or that it is frivolous enough—whatever you most need, I hope it has been achieved.

Thank you, Francis, for putting up with my powder room tale.

With love and fervent wishes for your speedy recovery,

Joan

FROM THE DESK OF MRS. IMOGEN FORTIER

April 23, 1965
Lake Forest Park, Wash.

Dear Miss Bergstrom,

I considered writing this letter by hand but have decided my clumsy mistakes on Immy's typewriter are preferable to my ~~indeviph~~ ~~index~~ indecipherable chicken scratch. As for my strike-throughs, they in turn are ~~prfer~~ preferable to the smudgy mess I make on the page with correction fluid.

Immy insists I write the following with quotation marks so you will ~~knoq~~ know these are her exact words:

"Oh Joan what a divine adventure you're having. Mrs. Brown sounds like an exceptional woman, and I'm thrilled about your ~~cookkbok~~ ~~cokbokk~~ cookbook idea and the romantically named Henrietta Neatrour. You ~~muxt~~ must send more details as soon as you have them. I know your ~~cookbk~~ cookbook will be a success. Francis, make sure to add an exclamation point ~~tto~~ to that sentence. You have enlivened our lives with your adventurous palate even though Francis spends so ~~mch~~ much time in the ~~kkitchen~~ kitchen now his ~~borthers~~ brothers call him the little missus. You don't mind, do you, Francis?"

I (Francis) ~~an ak~~ am adding my own words to assure you that I don't mind my brothers' ~~teass teasinnh~~ teasing because they always eat my food and ask for more so I am able to hold this over their heads. Also, I don't mean to be forward and interject myself into your personal correspondence with Immy, but what she says is certainly ~~trud~~ true. Our life together is richer because of you. Thank you.

With warm regards,

Francis Fortier

April 30, 1965
Los Angeles, Calif.

Dear Immy and Francis,

 Your earthquake is all over the news. Please send a quick note to let me know your house and cabin are still standing.

With love,

Joan

From the Desk of Mrs. Imogen Fortier

May 7, 1965
Camano Island, Wash.

Dear Joan,

Once again I'm dictating a ~~lttt~~ letter to Francis who promises to convey my words with accuracy but less literal precision than his last effort. When ~~hr~~ he read it back to me I laughed so hard I had to take two Bayer. (Francis here. In my defense I was concentrating ~~in~~ on typing and did not ~~reak~~ realize~~d~~ what I had done until I was finished. I offered to ~~retpe~~ retype it, but Immy wanted me to send it as is.)

My right eye, or ~~rqther~~ rather the abandoned space ~~wnn~~here (Francis here. I've decided to strike out letters rather than full words when it makes sense to do so; ~~o~~perhaps it will make this more readable. I'm starting this sentence over.) My right eye, or rather the ab~~b~~andoned space where my r~~o~~ight eye once lived, is bandaged, and my left eye is blurr~~t~~y with the fatigue of doing double duty. Just sitting up tires me. But I told ~~G~~Francis I want to assure you myself that although the earthquake rattled us for nearly a ~~mnute~~ minute~~s~~, we're fine.

Francis was already at work since the university's electricians~~sss~~ go in early on Thursdays, and my sister-in-law Irene was on nursing duty with me. We were listening to Frosty Fowler on KING ra~~dd~~dio. Mr. Fowler broadcasts from the top of the Space Needle, so you can imagine ~~xcv~~ the shock in his voice when his sky-high perch began to sway, interrupting Connie Francis serenad~~fi~~ing the morning traffic. What a trouper that man is. He kept ~~rgght~~ right ~~of~~ on reporting and taking calls about fa~~llll~~en chimneys and such from all over the city.

Fortunately for us the earthquake was centered to the south of Seattle, and both Lake Forest Park and Camano Island are to the north. It wa~~ss~~ frustrating not to be able to go out to the island with Francis to check on things right away. His brothers went with him while Hazel stayed and kept an eye on me. Funny how many idioms include the word eye. I never noticed before. Eye opener. Apple of my eye. Bird's eye view. Keep your eyes peeled. In it up to your eyeballs. (Francis here. I think I'm getting the hang of this. An entire paragraph with only one mist~~t~~ake. ~~Spke~~ Spoke too soon.)

This new situation of mine has deepened my already enormous appreciation for how much kindness and love I have i~~m~~n my life. Between Hazel, my cousin Pauline, my sisters-in-law, ~~rest~~cetera, etcetera, I'm well-fed every day, and they make sure I'm never alone to trip or feel sorry for myself. My niece Kit has visited twice, and she even attempted to ba~~k~~ke me a coffee cake. She hates her kitche~~m~~n as much as she loves her horses so I consider this an especially thoughtful gift. The cake, by the way, will ma~~d~~ke an excellent doorstop.

Mr. Pellegrini has been te~~mm~~nding my garden and cheering me up by antagonizing Francis with loud argu-ment~~tt~~ts about the merits of cooking with olive oil over butter (Francis here. Butter is superior.), and Mr. Luke is reading chap~~pp~~ters of a thought-provoking book called Garden Cities of To-Morrow into a magnetic tape re-corder. He brought the ~~wole~~ whole contraption to the house, which prompted Hazel with her never-ending sup-ply of cottage cheese and salmon molds ~~so~~ to contact an organization for the blind. They sent over an Agatha Christie. I ~~e~~read it years ago, b~~i~~ut hearing it is another experience entirely. Then I have ~~yy~~you down in Califor-nia sending me descriptions of your thrilling life as you prepare Ma~~d~~dam President Frida to meet the world.

Today is the first day my doctor has allowed me to come to the island. Francis has me propped in a re-clining ch~~q~~air in front of the big window with the front door open and an agreeable breeze streaming in ~~throgh~~ through the screen. While I can't see clearly I know exactly what is happening outside. S~~o~~pring is well underway, and the wild cherry trees are in full bloom. The fields ar~~t~~e filled with darling violets and buttercups, and the sides of the road lined with the blossoms that will become berr~~r~~ies in the summer heat. I know from the weather report that a crisp spring light is shining down on the navy blue water of Saratoga Passage, and my view, whether I can see~~e~~ it~~t~~ or~~rr~~ not, will remain unchanged. I wrote to you once about the comfort I find in that. This remains ~~rue~~ true.

The sun will set soon, and Francis has filled the cabin with the war~~n~~ming smell of the omelettes he has perfected. (Francis here. I filled them with fresh tomato puree and sprinkled grated ~~W~~Swiss cheese over the top before putting them under the broiler.) And so with a satisfied stomach and a heart filled with gratitude, tonight as I lie in bed before~~ee~~ I fall to sleep, I will do as I have done every night since the surgery~~y~~. I will smile my way into my dreams as I think about the countless ways my life is blessed.

With love,

Immy

May 9, 1965
Snohomish, Wash.

Dear Miss Bergstrom,

My name is Irene. I am Imogen's sister-in-law. I am very sorry to send you this news. Two nights ago Imogen passed peacefully in her sleep. She spoke of you often and treasured your friendship. She kept all of your letters in a special lacquer box. Francis requested that I send you the box and letters, as well as the layettes she knitted for your baby. He also found a sealed envelope addressed to you, which I am enclosing.

The funeral will be held on May 14 at the Lutheran church on Camano Island. The burial will take place at the Lutheran cemetery.

With warm regards,

Irene Corskie

FROM THE DESK OF MRS. IMOGEN FORTIER

April 8, 1965
Camano Island, Wash.

Dear Joan,

I have driven out to the island by myself to write this letter to you the day before my surgery. If you receive it, that means I'm no longer here on earth, or at least not aboveground anymore. I will miss life, make no mistake about it, but the portion that was allotted to me was a generous gift, made all the better because you were a part of it.

Also, if you receive this letter it means that another letter was posted. It was written to Mateo. Don't be mad at me! I didn't tell him about Frida. Those splendid beans aren't mine to spill. What I did say, or rather ask, is that when you come to him, would he please listen to you with his heart.

Go to him, Joan. You must! I'm not able to live anymore, but you can live for me. You can make new adventures. Taste new flavors. Love Mateo as fully as is possible. Create a new kind of family and change the way the world thinks about what is right and wrong.

Regale Frida with tales of her Aunt Immy who wore a crown of kelp and walked the streets of Paris at three a.m. Your loving and dearest friend, until we meet again, Immy

P.S. I assume you will receive the many layettes I made. I admit I got carried away, but knitting turned out to be more enjoyable than I had thought it would be. Apologies for the dropped stitches.

May 13, 1965
Los Angeles, Calif.

Dear Francis,

I send my respects and share your sorrow at Immy's passing. She was my cherished friend, and I will miss her beyond measure.

Please thank your sister-in-law for her kindness in sending the box of letters and the layettes. If there is anything I can do to help you honor Immy, I am at your service.

With warm regards,

Joan Bergstrom

May 15, 1965
Los Angeles, Calif.

Dear Immy,

Your service was yesterday. You once mentioned in a letter your love of wildflowers. I hope you liked the bouquet I had sent and that they didn't cause a fuss because they weren't waxy calla lilies.

I cried last night for a long time. I miss you so much already. I ache to think that I am going to miss you for the rest of my life. When I woke this morning my face was red and more swollen than usual. I had to wait for cool water and cucumbers, along with a cup of coffee, to do their tricks before I drove to Mateo's house. I parked up the street so I could walk toward it and hopefully see him before he saw me.

Dazzling jacaranda petals covered the sidewalk like a carpet of amethyst velvet. It always amazes me how the trees sit so quietly, unnoticed all spring, until one day it feels as if every single one throughout the city bursts with blossoms at the exact same second. The geraniums were in bloom in their coffee cans in Mateo's yard, and I could hear the sound of his smoothing plane gliding over a piece of wood. I followed it around the side of the house to his workshop. He was bent over a project listening to the noontime concert on KFAC.

I have always admired his ability to concentrate, and I was especially thankful for it at that moment. Oh, Immy, looking at the strength of his hands, I wondered how I ever thought I could live without him. I whispered his name. He turned around. At the sight of my brimming maternity dress, he didn't recoil or blink in confusion. He just said, "I suppose it will be a while before we're able to ride our bicycles up the coast again."

He asked me to marry him. I said yes.

He knew about your passing from the letter you sent. His grief is as heavy as mine. He credits you for my courage to return to him.

Along with kelp and Paris, I will tell Frida, when she learns about the Cuban crisis in school, how her Aunt Immy mentioned Elizabeth David in a letter, and that reminded me of a recipe for risotto alla Milanese I had long wanted to try. So I made it for dinner and invited the neighbors, and their carpenter who happened to be working at their house. I will tell her you are the reason her father and I met.

I don't know what I am going to do with this letter, but I had to tell you that Mateo and I are getting married. It's not real otherwise.

With love, your friend, always and forever,

Joan

June 25, 1965
Los Angeles, Calif.

Dear Immy,

My instincts were right. I had a girl. She was born last week with robust lungs and beautiful golden brown fingers and toes. We named her Immy Frida Rodriguez, and she is the most adorable baby in the world dressed in the sweaters, caps, and booties made by your own hand.

Please forgive me, but I'm not going to write to you again. It simply hurts too much.

With the greatest of pain and the greatest joy,

I know you, and only you, will understand what I mean,

Joan

August 6, 1966
Los Angeles, Calif.

Dear Francis,

    I am sending an advance copy of my cookbook, which will be published by The Macmillan Company in the fall. I hope the vignettes I have shared about Immy bring you the same comfort that the memories of her friendship bring me.

With warm regards,

Joan Bergstrom

P.S. I have enclosed a blend of Provencal herbs (marjoram, rosemary, thyme, and oregano) that Mateo and I grew in our garden and dried in our hot summer sun. Immy once told me how you use this mixture to enhance your voyage on the high seas of French cooking. I hope you are still embarking on such voyages. They were a source of great happiness for her.

COOKING CALIFORNIA STYLE

JOAN BERGSTROM

for Immy,

with

love & saffron

Author's Note

At the start of the pandemic, when Los Angeles issued its Safer at Home emergency order, I found myself drawn to my desk each morning, writing a story as a gift for two friends, Janet Brown and Barbara Hansen. I wanted to create a balm, a small antidote for the disorienting and uncertain times we were living through. It turned out that writing about Immy and Joan was also a salve for me because it allowed me to lose myself in reflections on women I admire and love.

In 1995, when Janet and I left the Elliott Bay Book Co. in Seattle, me to teach English in Vietnam and she to teach in Thailand, we began a correspondence that grows stronger and more meaningful each year. As Immy wrote to Joan, "When a new experience comes into my life, it doesn't feel real anymore until I've shared it with you." I can say the same thing about Janet, and it is our quarter-century of writing to one another that drives the spirit of *Love & Saffron*.

Joan is inspired by Barbara, a James Beard Award–winning food journalist with a ravenous culinary curiosity. Barbara wrote regularly about international flavors back in the 1960s, long before it was fashionable to do so, and her "Border Line" food column at the *Los Angeles Times* is historically significant for chronicling the city's unsung Mexican food for an English-speaking audience. For years we met up at the Original Farmers Market for Bob's doughnuts and coffee, and I'm thankful for how generous she's been about letting me "steal" details of her life from those morning conversations.

Then there is Immy: my Great-Aunt Emma. She and my Great-Uncle Frank owned the very cabin Immy and Francis live in on Camano Island. Great-Aunt Emma died of cancer when I was a young child, and I have gauzy memories of summer visits to the cabin and a loving woman who intrigued me. She was a down-to-earth Pacific Northwest soul who lived within the boundaries of her known world, but she was also the owner of mysterious treasures like the copy of an exotic magazine called *The New Yorker* that I still have to this day.

As I was working on *Love & Saffron*, I wanted it to be a book that could be read and savored in one nourishing sitting. The result is this gentle story about friendship, food, and love that managed to find its way beyond its original audience of Janet and Barbara. My thoughtful agent paired me with an equally thoughtful editor whose understanding of *Love & Saffron* on a spiritual level continues to fill me with gratitude. As we embarked on the editorial process, we wondered about Immy's column—the one that inspired Joan to reach out to her. It felt important to us to know what was in that column, and so I wrote it. While we decided that it wasn't the right way to begin Immy and Joan's story, I want to share it with you in the hope that you will enjoy this glimpse into that part of Immy's life.

NORTHWEST HOME & LIFE

The Magazine of
Pacific Northwest Living

OCTOBER 1962

Letter from the Island

BY IMOGEN FORTIER

ANOTHER HAPPY SUMMER has come and gone here on the island, and with it our long, ambling days and their glorious sunsets. The crab pots are headed for hibernation in the rafters of the boathouse, and fair-weather neighbors are shuttering their cabins all along the beach.

I adore this back-to-school season, even though it's been decades since I was a fresh-faced schoolgirl east of the mountains in Toppenish. The mingling of nostalgia and crisp autumn air stirs something bone-deep inside me. The nostalgia is stronger than usual this year, I suppose because this month's column marks my tenth anniversary writing "Letter from the Island." I was in my ripe forties when I began, and now I'm nearly sixty. Time certainly passes on its own terms, doesn't it?

The cabin is enjoying a well-earned rest after months of in-laws and cousins, old friends and new. Without the flurry of others, I puzzle over what I can write to compete with the summer's excitement. I'm still marveling that my niece Kit persuaded me to try waterskiing. Who cares that I looked absurd in my bright orange bathing cap? Or that I spent more time in the drink than on top of it? For a few thrilling moments I was a gull skimming the salty wake. Every woman should know that feeling at least once in her life!

I'M TOLD THAT readers have enjoyed my cautionary tales of island living over the years, so I'll share my latest. Yesterday, Francis decided to clean barnacles and mussels off the buoy and mooring chain, and I had the entire morning to myself to hone my housekeeping skills. I've never understood the national penchant for spring cleaning. Why would anyone scour nooks and crannies right when all the doors are about to be flung open for summer? I'd be happy to lead a campaign to put autumn cleaning on the ballot. After all, that's when entertaining wanes and houseguests wipe their feet politely on the doormat rather than run in and out for Chex party mix and cold pop, spreading sand everywhere they go.

I pulled all the plates and glasses and pots and pans out of the kitchen cupboards. Where on earth did I get a Swedish butter curler, and what on earth did I intend to make with all those cans of cling peaches? While I got down to business with a bottle of Pine-Sol, I had my annual conversation with the deluxe cake-decorating kit I bought with Green Stamps who knows how long ago. I assured it that this year I *will* learn to use it, and I returned it to the cupboard to join the ten rolls of Con-Tact paper I keep meaning to line the drawers with. The road to you-know-where, etc. etc. We can't all be June Cleaver!

I was enjoying a bracing camaraderie with my Brillo pad, removing the summer's cigarette smoke and bacon grease from the walls, when Francis came in to tell me the tide was unusually low and didn't clams sound good for dinner? Indeed! I threw off my rubber gloves, jumped into my rubber boots, and grabbed a bucket and spade. Down where the pebbles meet the sand, I was delighted to see the lively mollusks squirting up water like the International Fountain at the Seattle World's Fair. Unfortunately,

I leaped into an especially soft spot, and the next thing I knew, my boots were stuck as if someone had glued me in place.

"Hold still!" Francis shouted, but I've always been better at the love rather than obey part of our vows. The more I thrashed about, the worse the situation became. I slipped sideways in a tangle of kelp, and the next thing I knew I was wearing a briny crown. While a smug heron stood effortlessly on top of the mud and watched on, I feared Francis might have to rig some kind of winch to pull me out, or at the very least I'd have to abandon my boots. But after much tugging and not a small amount of creative cursing, he managed to free me. And despite my effort to sabotage our grubbing, we still finished with a pail full of butter clams.

Back at the cabin, Francis dubbed me Queen Slips-a-Lot because, I confess, this is not the first time this has happened to me. He made me a sash out of old *Parade* magazine pages, and I carried the title proudly as we ate half the clams with butter, lemon, parsley, and Tabasco for dinner in front of Lawrence Welk. The rest I left in a bucket of cold water with cornmeal to clean out the sand. Cribbage before bed, and Francis skunked me again. Then to sleep and up for a breakfast of fried eggs and clam hash.

AFTER FINISHING MY kitchen cleanse, I'm now spending a lazy Sunday in one of our old wooden chairs on the patio watching the water. Sandpipers make their playful "cheep-cheep" sounds as they scurry by, and a handsome cormorant floats out on a log, its sleek black wings spread open to the sun. The nostalgia I mentioned earlier nestles sweetly in my thoughts of summers past. Camping out in the drafty old one-room cabin before we replaced it with this newer one. The look on Francis's face the time he caught a nine-pound humpy. Mornings radiant with the days to come, sparkling starlit nights, and ten blessed years of sitting in this spot with my notebook and pen, writing this column before taking it home to type and mail to my editor.

I've always loved basking in memories as they curl into each other like kittens I once saw sleeping in a thick quilt on a friend's back porch. And yet, at the same time, I'm eager for the season ahead. When we come out next weekend, I'll bring Gravensteins from our tree in town and put myself to work making apple butter. The bigleaf maple and paper birch are changing fast, and we'll return to brighter colors and plenty of wonderful leaf piles to kick through on our morning walks. Francis stacked wood in the boathouse, ensuring we're ready for the winter storms and their Luddite hostility toward electricity. I don't mind the inconvenience, though, since there are few things more exhilarating than gusty days with crashing waves and whitecaps.

AS FOR THE caution in the tale that I promised, I haven't forgotten about it. To make a short story long, as I'm known to do, when you are out clamming, the instant you begin to sink in the muck, stop immediately and back up the way you came. Francis just read over my shoulder and asked me to emphasize: Do not thrash!

Until next month,
Your faithful island correspondent,
Mrs. Imogen Fortier

A Meal with Joan and Immy

The first time I read Barbara Hansen's *Cooking California Style*, I felt as if I had found a delicious time capsule containing a memoir and travelogue all in one. I had met Barbara a few times, but after devouring her cookbook, I knew I must become friends with her: her sense of adventure, her culinary curiosity, her genuine love of foods from other cultures! The friendship I longed for developed, and then, years later, came *Love & Saffron*, and Joan, who was so richly inspired by Barbara. So ... if Joan was going to serve Immy a meal from *Cooking California Style*, what would it be? Together, Barbara and I curated this small menu the two friends could share over a bottle of rosé—reminiscent of the "vin rose" Joan and Mr. R took away from Pea Soup Andersen's Old Country cellar on their day trip to Solvang. The recipes are presented, with Barbara's introductions and notes, as they were in *Cooking California Style*, with slight changes for clarity. Our additional notes can be found in italics after each recipe.

In the words of Francis's culinary heroine, Julia Child: *bon appétit!*

FIRST COURSE

Guacamole Soup

Too many avocado soups are bland and unexciting, but nothing with a Mexican touch is ever dull, as this excitingly flavored, liquid guacamole will prove.

½ avocado

2 tsp. lemon juice

1 cup half-and-half

1–2 tbsp. coarsely chopped green chile

1 small clove garlic

3 tbsp. chopped brown-skinned yellow onion

2 tbsp. cilantro

1 cup light chicken stock

½ tsp. salt

This soup is made entirely in the blender. Start by blending the avocado with the lemon juice. Next add the half-and-half and blend again. Now add the chile, garlic, onion, and cilantro and blend again. Lastly, add the chicken stock and blend. Test for seasoning before adding the salt. If the chicken stock is salty, you may not need so much.

Serve the soup very cold with additional cilantro leaves as garnish. Makes 4 first-course servings.

NOTE: It is best to serve this soup on the day it is made and not to hold over.

Barbara used a fresh Anaheim chile, easy to come by when she wrote the cookbook and also known then as an Ortega chile. Because the skin is a little tough, it should be roasted and peeled before chopping. Canned chiles can be substituted. Canned Anaheims are simply called green chiles.

This recipe is light on avocado. I love avocado so I would use one (or even two) and cut back on the half-and-half. I would also add lime wedges for garnish.

Barbara suggests serving this with a very fresh bolillo (Mexican baguette), cut in half and lightly toasted, or French bread, sliced and lightly toasted, sprinkled with good California olive oil—picked up in Solvang if possible!

MAIN COURSE

Chayotes con Carne

Isla de Mujeres is a tiny, palm-trimmed island off the coast of Quintana Roo where you may go for a swim in the bluest of waters and come in, as I did, to a lavish meal featuring chayotes prepared this way.

2 large chayotes
1 brown-skinned yellow onion
2 tbsp. butter
1 cup stewed tomatoes, drained
¼ tsp. Mexican oregano
Pinch of ground cloves
Pinch of garlic powder
Salt
Freshly ground black pepper
½ lb. ground beef
½ tsp. taco seasoning mix
Grated Parmesan cheese

Cut the chayotes in half lengthwise. Remove the thin, flat seeds and boil the halves until tender, about ½ hour. Then scoop out the pulp, leaving the shells intact for stuffing.

Chop the onion and cook in 1 tablespoon butter. Add the tomatoes and sprinkle with oregano, cloves, garlic powder, salt to taste, and pepper. Stir in the chopped chayote pulp.

Brown the ground beef in 1 tablespoon butter and season with a little salt, pepper, and the taco seasoning mix. Combine the beef with the vegetables and heap the shells with this mixture. Sprinkle generously with grated cheese and bake at 350° for ½ hour. Serves 4.

It may be convenient to substitute Mediterranean oregano, but it's worthwhile to seek out the Mexican variety. While Mediterranean oregano is from the mint family, Mexican oregano is from the verbena family, which gives it citrusy notes, as well as a hint of anise.

If you are serving this for a light lunch, there is no need for accompaniment. If for dinner, it pairs nicely with a salad like the one included in this menu.

SIDE COURSE

One-Bean Salad

If you're bored with the tried-and-true three-bean salads, try this for a change. The one bean is the pinto, which is fundamental to Mexican cookery. Nopales are tender portions of cactus that are sold fresh or canned in little green dice in Mexican markets. I use canned nopales for this salad.

1 (15-oz.) can pinto beans
1 small brown-skinned yellow onion
½ cup canned nopales, drained

THE DRESSING:
6 tbsp. oil
3 tbsp. apple cider vinegar
1 clove garlic
½ tsp. salt
¼ tsp. cumin
¼ tsp. Mexican oregano
¼ tsp. freshly ground black pepper
Dash of cayenne

Lettuce leaves
Toasted tortilla chips

Drain and rinse the beans. Slice the onion paper thin and separate the slices into rings. Combine the beans, onion rings, and nopales in a bowl. In a small jar, combine the oil and vinegar, the garlic mashed in the salt, and the cumin, oregano, pepper, and cayenne. Cover the jar and shake until the dressing is well blended. Toss the vegetables with the dressing. Cover and chill, stirring occasionally. Mound each serving on a lettuce leaf and garnish with a tortilla chip. Makes 3 servings.

Back in the day, the oil used in a recipe like this one was Crisco or "salad" (vegetable) oil. Feel free to substitute olive oil—Barbara and I would!

Barbara also recommends this recipe for a party salad. Double the recipe and use about 2½ cups rinsed, diced, canned nopales. Gently toss the salad with slightly less than 1 cup dressing and marinate overnight. For serving, decorate with thinly sliced red onion, parsley, and fresh Mexican oregano. Serve with chips.

DESSERT

Dulce de Coco
(Coconut Dessert)

*The Pan American Restaurant in Los Angeles introduced me to
Cuban desserts, including this unusual combination of cream
cheese with a syrupy coconut topping. Any leftover topping will
keep almost indefinitely in the refrigerator and can be used in
many ways. I add a little to tropical drinks that I make in the
blender. You can also serve it over fresh fruit or ice cream.*

3 cups grated fresh coconut (1 medium coconut)
3 cups sugar
3 cups water
¼ cup light corn syrup
½ tsp. coconut extract
1 (8-oz.) pkg. cream cheese

To prepare the coconut meat, puncture the softest eye
of the coconut shell, drain out the milk, and crack the
shell. Pry out the meat and cut off the thin brown skin

attached to it. Grate the meat and pack it down when measuring.

Combine the sugar, water, and corn syrup in a large saucepan and bring to a boil. Add the coconut and boil gently, stirring frequently, for 1¼ hours, or until very thick. Remove from heat and stir in the coconut extract. Cool and refrigerate. You will have about 1 quart topping.

Divide the cream cheese into eight slices. Top each slice with a generous amount of the coconut mixture. Makes 8 servings.

NOTE: If you like lots of syrup, boil 1 cup water and 1 cup sugar and 2 tablespoons light corn syrup to a temperature of 220° on a candy thermometer. Flavor with a few drops of coconut extract and add as desired to each serving of dessert.

It's now possible to buy grated fresh coconut frozen in some Asian, Mexican, and Latin American markets; if you can find it, this will save you a lot of time.

The addition of coconut extract might seem redundant, but the extract will boost the flavor of the fresh grated coconut.

When making the syrup, keep a close eye on it, as it can thicken in less time than the recipe calls for.

Acknowledgments

Along with Janet, Barbara, and my Great-Aunt Emma, I want to thank:

My agent, Kate Garrick, for her patient support and genuine kindness. My passionate Two Roads publisher, Lisa Highton, for believing in my "real reader's book" and offering it a cozy home in the UK. Editorial assistant Charlotte Robathan for guiding me on my Two Roads journey with such graciousness and charm. Designers Sarah Christie and studiohelen for the vibrant and oh so brilliant UK cover. At Putnam in the US: My editor, Tara Singh Carlson, who connected with *Love & Saffron* in a way that exceeds my dreams. Editorial Assistant Ashley Di Dio for keeping the process running smoothly. My publicity and marketing Dynamic Duo: Kristen Bianco and Colleen Nuccio. Designers Katy Riegel and Monica Cordova for making the US version of my little book so pretty. The Putnam team cheering it on: Sally Kim, Alexis Welby, Ashley McClay, Leigh Butler, Tom Dussel, and Wendy Pearl. Boots on the ground: Kurtis Lowe for being such a generous champion of *Love & Saffron* and books, books, books! Cortney Kelley for bringing her radiant spirit to my author photo shoot.

My first *Love & Saffron* readers, whose encouragement nourished me: Naomi Hirahara, Susan Elia MacNeal, Colleen Dunn-Bates, Diana Chambers, Laurie Stevens, Connie DiMarco, Dana Sachs, Natalie Compagno, my kind-hearted sister-in-law Anita Vitale-Geisz, my beautiful cousins Jeanne Fay and Shelly Anton, and Aunt Pat Fay, who generously shared her love of Camano Island's seasons with Immy. My Pandemic Lifeline: Andrea Pastori, Vickie Hsieh, Sarah Spearing, Jenny Fumarolo, and Christie Kwan, who also drew the elegant spot illustrations for this book. My Dames: Connie Brooks, Alexi Drosu, Jen Bergmark, and Karen Briner. My Hummingbirds: Stephanie Santos, Grace Solano, Jessica Jimenez, and Jayra Acevedo. Sister-neighbors always Tammy Schmidt. Cousinsacrossthecountry Jen Lew. Roosevelt or bust Michelle Katz. Hollywood hippie Hilary Hearty. Look-Ha-Py-Py Natalie Gorum. Peeloo Charlotte Ashborn.

Because conversations over a meal can shape lives, even if it is Pietro's pizza: Elizabeth Goodwin. Because Pacific Northwest women are strong in spirit and loyal to the end: Sandie Ely, Wendy Arends, and Kris Landin. Because courage requires a gentle heart, and a gentle heart requires courage: Duyên Nguyễn, Keanakay Scott, and Gigi Breland. Because time and distance mean nothing when friendships are pure and true: Beth Branco and Hương Petkoska.

Barbara's mother, Anne Masters Hansen. Wally Costello, who bought the Camano Island cabin from my great-aunt and -uncle, and answered my endless questions about clams, mussels, bird life, and tides. Pete Speltz, credit for the vermouth is all yours.

Gramps, my eternal gratitude for starting me down the storytelling road. Mom and Dad, your kindness, curiosity, generosity, and unconditional love are the cornerstones of this book. Jules, my lobster, Delany Sisters until the end of time. Oliver, being your Auntie Kimbo is one of the greatest joys of my life. And Jim, my forever partner in dance parties, tiny wine, and The Mabes (AKA Barnacle Betty).

About the Author

Kim Fay is the author of two historical novels, the instant national bestseller *Love & Saffron* and *The Map of Lost Memories*, an Edgar Award Finalist for Best First Novel. She has also written a food memoir, *Communion: A Culinary Journey Through Vietnam*, a Gourmand World Cookbook Award winner. She created and served as the series editor for the innovative *To Asia With Love* guidebooks, and was a Hotel and Travel Editor for the travel, food, and lifestyle website, *Gayot.com*, for thirteen years. She is currently the Managing Editor for The Animation Guild's *Keyframe* magazine and website.